The Injury

ten stories

Anna Enquist

THE INJURY

ten stories

TRANSLATED BY

Jeannette K. Ringold

The Toby Press, *London & Connecticut*

First published in 2000 by
The Toby Press *Ltd, London*
www.tobypress.com

Originally published in Dutch as *De kwetsuur: tien verhalen*
Copyright © Uitgeverij de Arbeiderspers 1999

The right of Anna Enquist to be identified as the author of this work has been
asserted by her in accordance with the Copyright, Designs & Patents Act 1988

Translation copyright © Jeannette K. Ringold 2000

ISBN 1 902881 22 2 (C)
ISBN 1 902881 23 0 (PB)

A CIP catalogue record for this title is available from the British Library

Designed by Fresh Produce, London

Typeset in Garamond by
Rowland Phototypesetting Ltd., Bury St Edmunds

Printed and bound in Great Britain by
St Edmundsbury Press Ltd., Bury St Edmunds

Contents

The crossing

Jacob wakes up when the front door bangs shut. He hears the wooden wheels of the handcart bump against the cobblestones; the sound moves farther and farther away. It's pitch dark in the box bed. It stinks. Jacob spreads his legs carefully and feels the solid calves of Klaas. On his half. Gently he pushes against his brother. Klaas turns over and blows his foul night breath into Jacob's face. Klaas has transparent white eyelashes. The skin of his full lips is cracked and his mouth hangs open. The nightcap has slipped off and the curly blond hair lies against the pillow in clammy folds. My brother is almost twenty years old. He can't read and he stinks of fish, thinks Jacob. If he hit you, he'd break your neck. Last year, at the fair, he was the strongest man in the whole village. Yet he has to swallow before sticking his knife into a fish.

Reaching across Klaas' enormous thighs, Jacob pushes the box bed open with his feet. The wood creaks as the door swings slowly. A weak light falls into the room from the direction of the kitchen. Jacob climbs out of bed and tiptoes past the dark lumps that lie on the floor. The girls shouldn't wake up yet. Everyone should still stay asleep for a while, except him and his mother who is busy in the kitchen. She smiles when she sees Jacob. She says nothing. She has rolled up her sleeves and is rubbing her hands and her wrists with grease. Jacob sniffs. Fish oil. In the village they say his mother has airs because she doesn't want to let her hands freeze to bits like everyone else. His mother can read and also write. Under her scarf she has shiny black hair, just like Jacob himself.

"Has Father left yet?" he asks in a whisper.

"Just now. In this cold. The cart was full of frozen fish. He said you're to untangle the nets so they're ready when he comes back."

With her chin, Mother points to the scullery where a dark pile of rope lies on the floor. Jacob closes the door and stands next to the stove. He stares into the laundry kettle; white rags float slowly alongside each other.

"He wants to go out for flounder this afternoon, while the ice lasts."

"Mother, Mum," says Jacob, "are we still going to read today? Please?"

With her shining hand she strokes his hair; he smells fish, grease and soap. He closes his eyes.

"Tonight. When you're back with flounder."

In the scullery Jacob has a secret hiding place at the bottom of the box with old fishing-gear. That's where his notebook is. He licks the tip of his pencil so that the letters will be black and heavy.

"It is Saturday, January 13. In the year 1849. Father has gone to the market. We are going to go out for flounder by hacking a hole in the ice and setting out nets, and I don't want to. The whole sea is ice. I am sixteen years old. No one knows that I will become a shipbuilder, like Katrien's father."

Klaas stumbles in and slips into the clogs that stand next to the door. Jacob quickly sits down on top of his notebook and fiddles with the cold brown rope of the tangled nets. Klaas fumbles with his hand in his trousers and pushes open the door to outside. A moment later Jacob hears splashing in the courtyard.

3

"Pissed a hole in the ice," says Klaas when he comes back in. "You've got to spread them out first, the nets, otherwise you see nothing. Outside, it's too dark in here."

Jacob makes a face at his brother's back. Then he puts away the notebook and starts dragging the tangled rope outside. Against the wall there is a steaming yellowish stain in the ice.

Jacob gets such cold fingers from checking the nets that he has to go and stand by the stove every other minute.

The girls are sitting at the table, sorting beans. Klaas has left to do a half day's work at the slipway before Father returns. The clock sounds eleven and Jacob yawns.

Suddenly Father is standing in the kitchen. He waves his extended arms through the air and slaps them with force against his body. He stamps on the floor with his stocking-feet. All the fish has been sold, his wallet is bulging with coins, and he has brought city bread for them. Now we don't have to fish today, thinks Jacob. There's enough money. Now I can go and watch near the slipway; perhaps Katrien will be there, coming to visit her father, and will see me. Then together we'll look at the snorting horse that pulls the ship up the slope. Because it's so exciting she'll put her hand on my arm for a moment and I'll smell the scent of her muff.

4

"I'll give you the pan to take along so you'll have something to eat if it gets late," says Mother.

Because his clogs are too large, Jacob winds a double layer of cloth around his feet. Over that go the socks, and finally the clogs. Klaas scoffs at that. He just pulls his dirty socks onto his dirty feet. He stands steaming in his undershirt in the icy cold courtyard. He is flushed from running. With Father he puts the nets, the axes, and the heavy pounding block on the sled. Jacob follows with the sails.

When you stand on the dyke, there's ice as far as you can see, a bluish white plain on which the sunlight glitters. Here and there groups of people are standing on the ice, forming brown and dark red spots in the light. The thin air echoes with hammer blows of axes cleaving the ice, of fishermen repairing a boat and ice pounders in the distance.

Father and Klaas have pushed the sled off the dyke and are beginning to head towards the sun. Jacob squeezes his eyes into slits so that he no longer sees people, only white. And the towers of Amsterdam at the horizon. Now slip away, back into the kitchen. Father beckons, Klaas calls. Jacob lowers his eyes and sees that he's holding the pan of food. Carefully he steps on the ice-covered grass with his clogs, pushing the irons into the hard earth, and descends to the ice.

5

Flounder live on the sea-floor. It's an inquisitive fish which comes up to take a look when someone beats a drum. The sound pulses from the ice into the freezing water, vibrates through to the flounder's body, and the fish threads its way along the sound waves to the source of the rhythm. The net hangs beneath the beating stick.

Flounder-fishers stand the hacked-off slabs of ice upright around the hole so that no one will fall in accidentally. It looks as though small white houses are scattered over the ice.

"That's Beers's hole," says Father. He points to a large ice castle. "He'll be back soon. We're going farther on; there's too many people here."

Father and Klaas always walk slightly faster than Jacob, even though they have to pull the heavy sled because there isn't a good wind for the sail. Jacob drags his clogs step by step across the rough ice. He feels a cramp coming up his calves. Suddenly he has lost sled, Father and Klaas. They are nowhere to be seen. Jacob is standing on a blinding expanse and has lost all sense of direction. The Durgerdam dyke? The city towers? His undershirt pricks against his skin, and his breathing quickens as he slowly turns around. Then he sees in the distance two small figures with the sled appearing from behind a mountain of ice.

6

By the time he reaches the fishing spot, Klaas and Father are already hacking furiously. They take turns battering the ice with their axes until it cracks and yields black water. They have taken off their jackets; they are bare-armed and sweating.

Jacob comes closer to bring up the nets. He has put the pan of food on the sled. In the distance a clock strikes three times.

Nothing really starts until the nets are hanging in the water. Then you have to lug the heavy pounding block some distance away in order to start banging on the ice with it. Jacob can't keep it up for long although he does it with pleasure. He hammers to the beat of a song that he sings silently to himself. He keeps thinking of the flounder which he beseeches, bewitches and bewilders. They take turns. After the pounding hunt, the three of them pull the net onto the ice. Stunned, dozens of large, dark fish are placed on top of each other in the sled. It's going well! Father peers across the expanse of ice. The sun sets.

"Beers is going back home. Porsius' lot have gone too. We'll do one more turn, they're coming so well today!"

Drag farther. The setting sun on the sandstone tower of Muiden. How far we are, thinks Jacob. When I get home, it'll be too late to read.

They have caught seven hundred fish; Jacob has kept the tally. With their backs to the stack of flounder, they are sitting on the edge of the sled, eating out of the pan. The banging of wood on ice keeps ringing in Jacob's head. It must be almost midnight, sleep tugs at his body. He sticks the spoon in his belt, he doesn't want any more.

Slowly they pull the very heavy sled over the ice. Father walks ahead with the lamp; Klaas and Jacob lean into the towing rope and drag their catch steadily in the direction of the light on the dyke. Soon to bed, thinks Jacob, take off the cutting rope, take off the cold clothes. Sink into a deep, deep sleep.

Father stands still. He lowers the lamp, silently. Suddenly Klaas and Jacob see why: between the ice and the dyke lies a wide strip of black water. Jacob gets tears in his eyes when he realizes that his box bed is out of reach. His calves are so tired that he can't stand any longer. "The ice is drifting," says Father. "We have to go on. See if we can get off at Uitdam."

Klaas starts turning the sled by himself. Father pulls Jacob up.

"Come, my boy. With such a fine catch we can keep going for a while. You take the lamp."

Like oxen under a yoke, the big men drag the sled. But wherever Jacob lets his light shine, the deep, black crack always shimmers back at him. Across from Uitdam they sit down for a moment.

"To the south," says Jacob. His voice sounds thin and weak through the dark. "If the ice has drifted away from the east coast, then maybe it has pushed against the southern dyke."

Father nods. The food is finished. There is no wind, no sound except for the scraping of the sled over the ice and the rasping of irons of the clogs. They walk in the direction of Muiderberg. It's day. They hear the bells of Naarden. A black ribbon lies between them and the shore line. Without a word they turn around, towards Marken.

Day turns into evening. Jacob is no longer tired.

Thoughts race through his head. The sled is too heavy, the flounder must go back into the sea. It's Father's fault. He who fishes so greedily will be punished. He is doomed to wander over the ice for days and nights, without hope of returning home. Mother will be worried; it has already been Sunday, and they were not there. The flounder has to go back. Then the ice will close up and we can go ashore.

Father won't hear of it. The catch is his; he wouldn't dream of offering up the flounder. In the middle of the night they try to sleep between the sails, next to the loaded sled, pressed against each other like the fish.

When Jacob wakes up he is alone. He sits up and bends his stiff legs. A few feet away Father and Klaas are on their knees. They have bent their heads and hold their caps in their hands. They are praying.

With his arms full of flounder, Jacob walks to the edge of the ice. He lets the fish slide into the water. Father screams when he sees what Jacob is doing. Father doesn't want it, and yet it happens. Without a word Klaas comes to help Jacob. Together they carry away the fish. Father sits on the sled; he keeps his eyes closed.

They keep fifty fish. To eat, with ice scrapings to drink. It isn't real; it's a dream; soon it will be over.

9

The sled glides easily over the ice. At a fast pace they walk toward Naarden, where there is water. Back to the north, where the ice creaks dangerously and threatens to give way unexpectedly under their weight. Three days have passed; in his mind, Jacob counts off each day on a finger. Tonight he will concentrate on the ring finger of his right hand. That means: Tuesday. In the distance lies Nijkerk, inaccessible behind a belt of broken ice. It rains. With axes Klaas and Jacob hack a hollow in the ice.

When it is filled with water, they slurp from it, on their knees, like animals. They eat raw fish. Jacob retches. Father has been silent all day. They take him between them under the sail. Father is cold. Jacob concentrates on the little finger of his right hand.

10

The fog is so thick that Jacob doesn't know if it's morning yet. He wriggles out of the sail to go and pee. The ground moves and he screams with fright. This wakes Father and Klaas. There is no ground; there is an ice floe which is surrounded by water. The three of them stand with their sled. They are floating. As if on a boat without a rudder.

The wind rises but the fog remains. Ice floes roll on the water and collide, break off, push past each other. Klaas walks around on their own floe, kicks away other ice fragments; with the broken-off mast of the sled he tries to pole in the water that's too deep. He can't sit still. He has to keep doing things. Because he's stupid, thinks Jacob. Just let the wind push them; soon the flood tide will come which will push them back. It's better not to move; it's better to wrap yourself in the sail and breathe against the stinking canvas. Drops form on it that you can lick. I'll never become a fisherman. I'll marry Katrien and I'll become a shipbuilder and every day I will write in a parchment copybook. On Saturday I'll pay Klaas his wages in small change. After that I'll go and eat roast pork with Katrien and her father.

Father is crying. We have to do penance, he says. The flounder offering was insufficient. Now Father wants to offer himself.

Klaas nods. The situation is hopeless. They will drown no matter what, sooner or later. In that case rather now, together.

Father and Klaas sit at the edge of the ice and look into the water. There lies their destiny. Father motions Jacob to come closer. It is time.

Despite the cold, Jacob begins to sweat. He has jumped up and wants to speak, but his voice remains stuck in his throat. There is a strange feeling in his stomach. He thinks of his little finger, the fifth day. There are big holes in Klaas' socks through which his red heels can be seen. Father has lost an iron from his wooden shoe.

"Idiots," Jacob shouts, "you're idiots! With the three

of us at the edge the floe will tip over. You are fools! Giving up, calling it quits, that's impossible. You can't even swim, but I can! And write, I can do that too. I don't want to die, I'm not going to die! Never!"

"God's hand, Jacob, God's hand is pushing us to the North Sea," says Father. "We have to surrender."

"Not at all," shouts Jacob. "The tide is turning, we may be washed ashore, you just don't know, the wind will turn, there's land everywhere, we have a chance. I don't want to. I won't go along with this. You jump in yourselves. Not me. I want to go to Mother!"

Klaas turns his head from one to the other. When he looks at Father, Klaas seems about to be sucked into the water; when Klaas turns to Jacob, it's as if he wants to stand up and do something.

12

Jacob sits down on the sled and starts to fillet a flounder. He places the pieces of boneless flesh next to each other on the edge. With the point of his knife he sticks a strip of flounder in his mouth. He starts chewing slowly and looks into the distance.

Like a dog, Klaas has sat down in front of Jacob on the ice and has eaten the prepared bites. Silently, Father has rolled himself in the sail. Jacob breathes deeper. The danger has passed.

There's a storm. Jacob and Klaas stow everything they have under the sled: pan, axes, ropes, the pounding block. Close to each other they sit leaning against the sled; Jacob snuggles against Klaas' sturdy thighs. The middle finger of the right hand. Ships sail on the sea. They will save us. Father is asleep. Klaas is an ox which has to be driven. By me. So that we stay alive and I can kiss Katrien, later. Pain in my feet. Cold.

"I feel nothing," says Klaas. "Only that my clogs seem to have got too small."

They wake Father, after long consideration. Jacob gives him rainwater from the pan to drink, and Klaas tries to feed him a bit of fish. Jagged lightning strikes through the air and immediately afterwards the sky cracks from the thunderbolt. With eyes wide open Father stares ahead. The flounder slides out of his mouth and remains hanging on his stubbly chin.

13

"That's clever, with that pan," says Klaas.

"I also know what day it is," says Jacob. "Saturday. A week has passed. You learn that in school, to keep track of the time."

"I couldn't do that, sit on that bench. I'd rather work outside."

"Don't you want to read then? You will always need someone for these things. I can do them myself."

"We're all going to die," says Klaas. "Keep to your own kind, that's best."

Jacob says nothing. Idiot, he thinks, mindless hulk, millstone, fool.

The next morning the fog seems to lift somewhat. Jacob points at a dark spot on the horizon: the fat tower of Enkhuizen. Through the still air, city sounds reverberate towards them: the clock striking, a dog barking.

"Us too!" says Jacob. "Maybe they can hear us too!"

They hold their hands in front of their mouths like a bullhorn and scream. They bang with the pounding block and hammer on the pan with spoons.

It's evening and nothing happens. Father has turned his face away. He just lies there. Klaas is worn out from trying to attract attention. Eyes closed, he mumbles to himself. Jacob makes a face in contempt. Pray, hope and wait—why, for what? If the people of Enkhuizen don't see and hear us, why should God? Maybe we don't even exist anymore, maybe we only think we're here. Eat, we have to eat. It's a good day to catch fish. To work!

Father and Klaas are not interested, not even when Jacob points out the rapidly dwindling stack of flounder. Without help he can't manage to set out the net and, furious, he has to join in their resignation. Idiots, fools.

Jacob is counting on a change when it's a little finger day again, a Monday this time, a good day for a new beginning. The fingers of both hands have been used up. It can't last much longer. The wind picks up and becomes a storm, from the north, Jacob thinks. The ice floe flies like a ship across the water; it has to go somewhere because a ship doesn't just wander about. He doesn't think it strange when an island appears on the horizon.

"I see Urk," he says to his brother. "Put on your clogs, soon we'll be going ashore!"

An Urk fisherwoman will put him near her stove, will put Father in the box bed with a blanket over him and the doors closed, will come out with warm beer and currant cake, will pull him onto her lap and rub his cold hands warm and he will cry, hot tears that won't stop running. His feet are so swollen that he can't put on his clogs.

Holding their breath, they wait for the landing.   *15*

When the storm blows them eastward past the island, Jacob can't believe it. It's as if a strong arm is pulling him away from the stove. As if he really feels the cold for the first time.

Klaas has shaken his head and has crawled into the sail, dejected. Jacob nudges Father.

"May I come in the sail with you? I'm cold."

Father looks past Jacob and gives no answer. Jacob tugs at the sail, hard. Father rolls out and remains lying on the ice, motionless. Jacob wraps the canvas around himself and then lets himself fall back onto the sled, between the remaining flounder.

The following days race past in a daze. Jacob forgets which fingers are next and no longer figures out how the tides change. He stays rolled in the sail, in a half-sleep from which he rises sometimes for a moment when rain hits him violently in the face or when he feels Klaas's heavy body move. Three times Klaas awakens him and forces him to sit up. "A ship!" he says. "I see a ship, look!"

Jacob sees dark grey waves on which ice floes are floating here and there. He sees his brother's bare feet sticking through the frayed socks. He doesn't see what Klaas sees. In between the disappointments Jacob dreams that he rolls his father and his brother with difficulty to the edge of the ice floe and finally gives them a last push. A small wave splashes over the floe, air bubbles rise up for a moment and then the water is still and black.

It is light. Get up, otherwise I won't be able to again. Drink water from the pan. Eat. Jacob keep shaking the sail in which Klaas lies asleep until there is movement. Klaas opens his eyes.

"Father," says Jacob. "Come and look at Father."

Father lies stretched out on the ice with his arms wide. His head is turned so that the right cheek is touching the ice and the mouth is stiff and strangely crooked. Klaas tries to lift Father. That doesn't work. Whatever they say, shout or scream—Father doesn't understand. Klaas pushes a sliver of fish flesh between the crooked lips, and Father spits the food out again. He doesn't want to eat his brothers and sisters, thinks Jacob. Father has become a flounder.

Water surges over the floe.

"We're too heavy. We have to unload," says Jacob. "Get higher up. Float."

Klaas can no longer use his feet. That's just as well because he doesn't agree with Jacob. The pounding block is an heirloom, an indispensable tool. It's a crime to push that into the sea. Jacob does it, looking askance at Father. Lightened, the floe rises up a little.

Klaas shuffles closer on his knees and punches Jacob in the face. He blows with his burst lips, he spits and gurgles but can't say anything. Jacob pushes his brother aside and gets the nets. And the heaviest axe. And the clogs that have become too small. Everything has to go.

"Grrff," says Klaas. Must be a ship, thinks Jacob. I'm sitting on an ice floe with a flounder and an imbecile who sees ships. If I look up and it isn't true, I'll cry. I won't do it.

Brown sails. You can see the ropes. A man in black breeches walks to the forecastle. He has something in his hands.

Jacob looks around. A flag. Something that is noticeable. Klaas is wearing a red baize shirt. Take it off! He tears

17

the soaked cloth from his brother's back and ties the shirt by one sleeve around the mast that he sticks up between the planks of the sled.

Now pound on the pan and shout. They're coming. They see us. Me.

The ship makes a turn and becomes smaller. Almost no sound came out of me, thinks Jacob. And our flag disappeared in the fog. He rolls himself into the big sail to sleep.

It seems like spring. The air smells sweet and there is a pale sun that feels warm on his face.

The floe, thinks Jacob. It will melt. Father lies with his face half in the water. Jacob shrieks in his ear, but Father doesn't react. Jacob turns around to Klaas who sits on the sled with his bare chest. His feet are big as cabbages, dark red and black.

"Help, idiot!" screams Jacob at his brother. "Father is drowning!"

The flounder wants to go to the water. That's where he belongs. With undulating movements of his whole body, Father crawls ever closer to the edge of the ice. A crack becomes visible under his stomach. Startled, Jacob jumps aside, to the sled. Then the floe splits and the crumbling fragment slides with Father into the abyss. The ice block comes back up, bobbing. Not Father.

A view: houses are outlined delicately against the setting sun. A bridge like an arch over water. People walk back and forth over it. Someone leads a cow along on a rope. Schokland, thinks Jacob. He falls asleep.

It has been night. Now it is day again. A little finger day? What number? Klaas has fallen over. Something has come out of his mouth. Reddish. The liquid has caked in the stubbles of his beard. Jacob nudges him in the ribs with the handle of the remaining axe, but Klaas makes no sound, no gesture, no movement.

Eat. The rest of the last flounder. On the lookout, a hand above the eyes against the sun. A hill, on it a church, a convent. A harbor. Ships. Smoke from a chimney.

The fishermen of Vollenhove throw their hooks into the fragile ice floe. A sled, a body, a boy. They carry him into the main room of the lodging house that overlooks the sea. There a fire is burning. The doctor comes and unwinds the bandages from the legs. A lukewarm bath. Clean clothes. Half a bowl of soup.

19

Jacob lies in the dark room where the logs are still smouldering in the hearth. He stares through the window at the stars. I'm a hero, he thinks. I have survived the crossing. I pushed the ballast into the water and remained afloat myself. Read and write. Katrien will marry me because I can live and float. I crossed to the other side and I can never go back.

Jacob lies in the main room under the warm blankets and cannot sleep.

Based on: *An authentic story of the miraculous rescue of Klaas Klaassen Bording and his two sons, after drifting for fourteen days on the floating ice of the Zuiderzee; published by a Commission in Vollenhove for the benefit of those saved.* Printed in Zwolle by R. van Wijk, Anths. Zoon, 1849.

Hunger

"Hanna, would you go to the milkman?"
Silence. Rattling of coins in a tin can. The kitchen door.
"Hanna! Come here! Can't you hear me?" Hanna looks in
the bathroom mirror. She has undone her braid. She
smoothes the loosened hair along her cheeks, tilts her head,
and pulls down the neck of her sweater. She opens her eyes
wide and licks her lips. I hear you fine, she thinks, I'll go
if you're too stupid to remember the milkman. Such effort:
write down what you need in the little book, put money
in the tin, and place the empty bottles in the rack. Hang
the string out of the mailbox so that Kees can let himself
in. Every day the same and still she forgets it. Only a stupid
person like my mother could do that. "I'm coming," she

calls while braiding the hair behind her head. Right away
her face seems narrower. Like a child's, she thinks, like a
twelve-year-old's.

Her mother stands in the kitchen with a shopping
bag filled with empty milk bottles. She is wearing tennis
clothes, her fat red legs stick out from under the pleated
short skirt. Yuck. If I do now what she wants me to, thinks
Hanna, then I can go to the city with Dee this afternoon,
then she can't say no. Silently, she picks up the bag.

"Well," says old Mr Lievaert when Hanna enters the shop,
"did Kees miss your house?"

With arms akimbo, he stands behind the counter with
its milk bottles. He doesn't believe in Kees, thinks Hanna,
what a lousy father. Sends his seventeen-year-old son out
with that heavy cart and immediately assumes that he
doesn't do it right. "My mother had forgotten the string.
Two milks and one buttermilk. Please."

Kees looks a little like his father. Black curly hair.
Broad. But Mr Lievaert is grumpy and looks mean; Kees
is shy and looks friendly. I'm not allowed to associate
with him. The Lievaert boys haven't gone to school, says
mother, they have a different background. What's more,
they're Roman Catholic. Saying hello is allowed; making
small-talk next to the cart while looking at Kees' cold fingers
that stick out of the knitted fingerless gloves, that's not
allowed.

Straight-backed, Hanna walks home, the bag now on the right, now on the left. She pulls back her shoulders so that her breasts in the new bra stick out, under the buttoned coat. She is sweating. It's October but still warm. Next month she'll turn fourteen.

When she turns into her own street, she lets her shoulders drop again. Outside the neighbours' house she looks up at Deetje's room. Dee is peering out of the window. She is wearing the pink sweater; she has put on lipstick. Dee makes a grimace of disgust at Hanna and holds up the maths book. Questioning, Hanna holds up four fingers. Dee nods and looks back into the room.

At four o'clock they bicycle downtown. If your homework is finished, if you're back before six, if you don't do anything silly, says Mother. Deetje is almost fifteen, don't let yourself be dragged into anything, soon ripe soon rotten, Mrs Wester doesn't know what to do with her. Last year she had to repeat a grade, don't let that happen to you! We're just going to look in the department store, Hanna had said. Just one errand. We'll be back soon.

Over the drawbridge, through the archway, along the canal. Mist hangs over the water, and through the shop windows an unnatural glare falls on the rounded paving bricks. They lean their bikes against a tree and enter a white-painted door between large windows. It says CAFETERIA on the shop front. Underneath, in smaller letters, it says "Simon Lievaert and Son". Simon is the rich brother of Lievaert the milkman; he has an ice cream shop himself and bought the cafeteria for his son, for "Son", for Jaak who is standing by a deep-fryer full of boiling oil in a close-fitting white jacket; Jaak, who turns around slowly on his heels when he hears the door open so that his profile with the pointed nose, the cowlick and the ducktail is briefly silhouetted against the wall.

Dee places her folded windbreaker on a chair. Jaak looks at her breasts under the pink sweater. Hanna blushes. Actually, the cafeteria was meant for Jaak's brother Siem, the oldest. For when he finished his national service. He had to go to New Guinea for two whole years. Tanned by the tropics, he would have stood there among the French fries, but he tripped over a mine and lost his legs. Back in Holland they took him to a convalescent home. Hanna heard her mother whisper about it with Mrs Wester. The legs gone. She doesn't dare to think or ask about it.

Dee has turned on the jukebox. Jaak comes from behind the counter and brings bottles of coke. Dee wants French fries, Hanna shakes her head, no.

Everything about Jaak is pointed and narrow. His black shoes have sharp points. He looks at Hanna as he gives her the coke. He smiles. He winks.

At night in bed she talks to him. How lonely it is behind the deep-fryer. How awful to have a brother without legs.

He puts his thin, bony arms around her shoulders and his head against her head. Jaak, oh Jaak, sighs Hanna.

Dee hands out éclairs in the classroom. She has tied the scarf that Hanna gave her around her neck. In the evening Hanna may have dinner with her; a bit much, said Hanna's mother, but since it's Dee's birthday she has to let her go. Mrs Wester has made chicken and Mr Wester gives a speech at the table. They toast with Exota lemonade. After dinner, Dee's brother Arnoud has to leave for soccer practice. Mr Wester gives Dee money to get ice cream at Lievaert's. Dee and Hanna stand on the granite floor in the creamy white space. It smells of sugar. Mr Simon Lievaert, Jaak and Siem's father, has wrists that are as broad as his forearms and the palms of his hands. With his left hand he holds the ice creams while he operates the whipped-cream machine with his right. The machine makes a screeching noise, like a concrete mixer. One by one Mr Simon places the ice creams under the whipped-cream nozzle. On the dollop of cream he places a small wafer for a take-out.

The back wall of the ice cream parlour consists of sliding doors with leaded windows. When Mr Simon came into the shop, Hanna caught a glimpse of the back room: a lamp, dark carpets, a lady with grey, curly hair. That's where Mrs Lievaert sits, thinks Hanna, across from Siem in his wheelchair; they sit by the fire crying over the loss of his legs. Let the machines in the ice cream parlour shriek so that we can't hear anything.

A motor sputters on the street. Jaak stands in front of the shop window. On the back of his moped he has tied a sports bag, a black bag with the letters PAS. He raises a hand to greet his father and then, nodding his narrow head, to Hanna and Dee. Hanna feels her heart leap in her chest. Mr Simon smiles. "You can't hold him back," he says. "No matter what has to be done in the store, he has to play soccer. Sunday they play the number one team, an important game. I'll put them in a box for you, easier to carry. They're playing Unitas."

Pitying, he shakes his head. Unitas is Arnoud's club, thinks Hanna. White shirts with a nice blue collar. Probably not very good. You have to be with PAS, that's real soccer. Mr Simon continues talking. "Jaak is talented, even if I say so myself. If he doesn't get them in, no one does. He's the centre forward, you know; it all depends on him!"

Quiet for a moment, he watches his son leave on his backfiring moped and then sets the ice cream box on the counter. Dee pays.

When they stop off at the cafeteria on Friday after school, they encounter Jaak in conversation with three heavyset men. They are sitting at an iron table, eating French fries. The steel chair-legs scrape over stone and their voices resonate through the space. Hanna and Dee stand waiting shyly until Jaak looks up. He smiles.

"Unitas!" one of the men says scornfully. "They're ninnies. We'll flatten them!" The man moves his enormous legs. Hanna sees a pale piece of bare back between his sweater and his trousers. "We're counting on you, Jaak, are you up for it?" Jaak has grabbed two bottles of lemonade which he hands to Hanna. He looks outside, past the men and the girls.

"Yes," he says, "it starts when we practise on Thursday; I seem to get hungry. And once it's Sunday, I'm really hungry for the ball. I can't help it."

The men roar approvingly. "Just demolish those balls, Jaak, we'll do the rest!"

"What does PAS mean?" asks Dee when there is a moment's silence.

"Push And Shove, dearie, what did you think?"

"Of course not," says Jaak, "it's something with Solidarity in it. My father should know, he's a sponsor. Will you come and watch on Sunday? It's going to be a great game. A big crowd. On the first field, then you can be in the stands. Or don't you like soccer?"

Hanna nods. Suddenly she likes soccer more than anything.

How beautifully he said that, she thinks. Hunger for the ball. He has a hungry face too. And sweet eyes when he smiles like that. We have to go on Sunday. We have to.

Cauliflower. Sausages. When father talks, small bubbles of spit fly over the dish of potatoes. It's about school grades. About doing homework first and only then into the city with Deetje. About a grade that's not high enough. "You have the brains. I don't want you to cut corners!"

Hanna looks at the cut sausage on her plate. White specks, grey specks, pink specks. How can you be hungry for sausage? You're hungry for things that are very important, that you want so much that your stomach tightens and you become light-headed. That kind of hunger doesn't make you eat, it only makes you sigh.

Now, she thinks, right now. "You're right. Monday we have a big maths test, I'm going to study really hard for it. I can't go to Grandma's this Sunday, I'm going to do maths all day. Dee is going to help me, she took it last year."

"Grandma won't like that," says Father, "just do your work on Saturday. Sunday isn't meant for that."

"I'm doing it Saturday as well, but there's far too much. I have to practise a lot because I'm not very good at it. Not as good as Dee."

Father puts his fork and knife next to his plate. He makes stains on the tablecloth. His face has become red and you can hear him breathing. "Let her go," says Mother.

"I'll ask Mrs Wester if she can go over there on Sunday. Then we'll have some time to ourselves."

All day Saturday Hanna sits in her room. In her maths notebook she draws a heart. An arrow through it goes from "Hanna" to "Jaak". Childish. She tears out the page, crumples it up, pulls it back out of the wastebasket and cuts it into shreds. How proudly Jaak's father watched him go. But also a bit sadly. Maybe he was thinking of his oldest son, of the legs that remained overseas.

At the end of the afternoon the air has become completely grey. Dee drops by; they drink tea in the kitchen. "If it rains, it's called off," she says. "Then the game is cancelled. When that happens to Arnoud, he paces around the house cursing and kicking." Hanna is shocked. Everything arranged for nothing! That's impossible. It can't be. It won't be.

At night she hears the rain batter against the windows. All the drops land in the soccer grass, the field turns into a soft muddy goo on which no one can satisfy his hunger for the ball. She cries in her pillow. The game has to be held and she has to be there. She'll cheer him on; he'll play soccer for her, for her. Afterwards he'll be calm and happy, he will forget his halved brother by the heater, he will walk to her, spattered mud sticking to his clothes, he comes closer, he extends his arms to her, and then, and then—

When she wakes up there is a strong wind, but the rain has stopped. Her parents leave, father without a word and mother with a half-smile. "Are you going next door soon, Hanna?" Hanna nods. Strange that you believe real lies: she sees herself working diligently on maths problems with Dee. It's true, but not really. In the bathroom she puts on her mother's mascara. Why doesn't she know what I'm doing, thinks Hanna, why do I have to cry, after all I don't really want her to know what I'm doing. She bites her lower lip and carefully wipes the tears from her eyes with the corner of a towel. Then she undoes her braid.

There aren't very many people on the soccer field yet, it's too early. Right behind the entry gate a man in a small wooden booth sits smoking a hand-rolled cigarette.

"We're waiting," says Dee. Around the field is a ditch, and they sit down near it. On their coats, because the grass is still wet. Dee has brought along her lipstick and a mirror for Hanna. Now they both have soft pink mouths, and they light the cigarettes which Dee got from her brother. The smoke hurts Hanna's throat, but the smooth cigarette in her hand feels nice.

"Hello!" says Jaak. With the toes of his shoes on both sides of the moped, he keeps his balance on the brick pavement. Hanna hasn't seen him approach. Startled, she stands up. "You have to go in over there!" He points to the man in the booth who is selling tickets to the spectators who are trickling in. "These ladies are my guests," says Jaak. Dee and Hanna follow him. The man winks at Jaak and gives him a thumbs up.

When Jaak has disappeared to the dressing room in the low shed, Dee and Hanna climb onto the stand. Hanna shivers in her wet coat, a jet of icy air blowing along her back.

On the field, the Unitas players in a wide circle are kicking the ball to one another, in a set pattern. Whoever doesn't have a turn jumps or waves his arms. At a short command from the coach, the men trot off the field, one after the other, single file; their blue collars make a moving line like water undulating along a wharf.

Now the stands are full of people. Dee points at Arnoud who is standing near the line on the other side of the field. He won't betray them, she says, otherwise she'll tell that he smokes. The wind has blown the clouds apart and now and then the sun sweeps across the grass like a searchlight. The PAS men enter the field in small groups in their black clothes with yellow-gold print. Skipping, Jaak walks next to a tall man who is holding a form. Hanna breathes out and sits up straight. Very short shorts. Sinewy legs with black hairs. Is he looking? He looks, he waves. Confused, Hanna raises her hand, without smiling. The referee folds up the form and thrusts it into his breast pocket. He whistles, it starts.

Disciplined, the blue-and-whites pass each other the ball, stop it, and look before they kick it away. The blacks plunge like crazy bees in the supposed direction of the ball but keep getting there too late. They're older and heavier than the Unitas players. Boys against men, thinks Hanna. It isn't fair. Or is it? The men are stronger, and they have Jaak. They make a noise, they scream and roar so that the blue-and-whites are startled and let them get the ball. Under the grass the ground is soaked with water. Players slip and make fountains of spurting clay. When a black player crashes mercilessly into a blue-and-white one, the referee whistles. Hanna sees the man with the bare back from the cafeteria turning red. He wants to attack the referee, but his friends restrain him. Then he catches the opponents' free ball against his giant body. Jaak takes over; controlling the ball, he tears past player after player, turns and swerves and runs until he is at the goal. He pokes a defender in the stomach with his elbow, feints and shoots.

On the stands the spectators spring to their feet and cheer. The blue-and-whites raise their hands, but the referee whistles and points to the centre mark. Jaak runs back, black streaks of mud on his legs. He clenches his fists and raises them.

During half-time most people remain seated, but Hanna and Dee walk to the field. "Well?" asks Jaak as he goes past on his way to the locker room. Hanna nods. Her eyes shine.

She has unbuttoned her coat, as if she's just as hot as he is. "Just watch," says Jaak, "I'll hit a couple in before long!"

The players go to the wooden shed. They wipe their shoes on an upturned broom at the entrance. No one can enter, except the coach with a tray full of mugs of steaming tea. "You're allowed in the canteen," says Dee. "Arnoud is in there. Shall we drink something?"

"What butchers," Arnoud says indignantly. "They kick and push and that ref says nothing. That son of the milkman plays pretty well, I think."

"He's from the ice cream shop. He has his own store too. We sometimes go there." Hanna's face has flushed. She wants a cigarette. She wants to talk about Jaak as if she's the only one who knows him, as if he belongs to her.

The locker-room door opens and everyone pours outside. Hanna and Dee remain standing next to the line with Arnoud. On the other side stands Kees, the milkman's son; Hanna waves at him and he waves back. She sees his eyes turn to the entrance, she follows his glance and starts. Mr Simon Lievaert, the ice cream king, pushes his eldest son onto the field. He has to strain; the wheels slip in the mud, and when he slows down, the wheelchair gets stuck. Siem is gripping the arm rests with his hands. On his lap is a folded plaid blanket which hangs down in front. The foot rests are folded up. When the wind blows up the blanket, there is emptiness.

Kees runs towards them. He taps his cousin on the

shoulder and together with his uncle he drags the chair to the Unitas goal. Siem has pointed his leg stumps at the field. Simon and Kees flank him like soldiers on guard.

Across the field, Unitas has scored a goal. The blue-and-whites let out a short triumphant shout and quickly take up their positions again, shaking each other's hands while walking. A groan comes from the stands. The men in black have become restless and stomp through the clay like elephants. They run the blue-and-white boys down, push them aside and quickly kick them in the shins when the referee isn't watching.

"Cheating bastards," says Arnoud. "I'm leaving. I'll hear about it. See you!" Furious, he strides to the exit. The PAS coach walks along the sideline in a baggy outfit. "Get them!" he calls out. "Go on. Clobber them, Jaak, clobber them! It's got to go in!" The cigar stub between his fingers no longer burns. Panting, the coach watches his men.

Jaak's face is pale. His mouth is like a stripe between the thin cheeks. The ball is passed to him by an enormous kick from the man with the bare back; and he charges at the Unitas goalkeeper. The spectators scream, the people on the stands drum with their shoes on the wood, the noise is deafening. Jaak chooses a corner, quickly his eyes sweep the goal area, for a moment his eyes catch his brother's squat body, he kicks. Missed. Between wheelchair and goal-post the ball disappears into the ditch.

Mr Simon should leave, thinks Hanna. It's miserable for Siem to look at all these strong legs. And Jaak, how can he hit anything with such a sight? Tears of pity well up in her eyes. Handkerchief. She turns around and blows her nose.

When she looks again, she sees Jaak running doggedly to the goal. The spectators hold their breath, over the field falls a silence which turns into cheering when the ball smashes over the goalkeeper's head into the farthest corner of the goal. Everyone jumps up and yells. The men lift Jaak on their shoulders and carry him to the centre mark.

"Come on," says Dee, "we're going to the canteen. Nice and warm." They walk past the locker room. Steam curls up and the sound of jets of water and men's deep voices escapes from the high windows. In the distance Hanna sees the broad, bent back of Mr Simon pushing his son disappear along the road. It's already getting dark. The inside is lit by weak light bulbs. The man who sold tickets stands behind the bar next to a woman in a checked apron. The windows are steamed up. Kees is drinking beer. They go over to him. On the walls hang photos of soccer teams. Dee wants beer too. Hanna waits.

Jaak's hair is wet. He has combed it straight back, but here and there a curl breaks loose. He shakes Kees' hand and throws his arms around Dee and Hanna. The warmth of his armpit. His hard ribs. They drink. Dee sits on a high stool; she has pushed her knees against Kees and swallows the beer in big gulps. Hanna listens to the sound of their voices; they scream with laughter, why, about what? Jaak keeps his arm around her shoulder and with his free hand he lifts the glass. Amidst the noise, the thumping of the radio and the thick blue smoke, Hanna creates a crystal-clear focus of attention on Jaak's face. Dark, fine eyebrows above the light eyes. The mouth. Shiny white teeth, the pointed tip of the tongue.

"We're going out for a moment, I'm boiling in here." He leaves his hand on her shoulder. Weak with laughter, Dee leans on the bar with her upper body. Gently Jaak pushes Hanna to the door. Everywhere they go, men call out "Jakey, Jakey!" They raise their thumbs and grin.

36   Is it evening already? It seems as if time doesn't exist. The path along the canteen and the locker room is lit by a streetlight. Across the field the stands are like a dark wall. Jaak presses Hanna against him. She throws her arm around his waist, she feels his hard body against her chest. Under the streetlight he stands still, he turns to her, smiles, and turns his head towards her face.

The canteen door flies open, and a man roars: "Goal, Jakey!" Grinning, he disappears into the dark. "Pain in the ass," says Jaak. "Probably has to piss."

The locker-room door is ajar. "Come quickly," whispers Jaak. He pulls her inside, she trips over the up-turned broom and crashes against him. They fall down on the hard floor, a shooting pain tears sharply through her elbow and for a moment everything turns black.

She lies on the stones. Sand, mud, it feels wet on her back. Through the transom window, the yellow light of the streetlight shines in. An overturned soccer shoe lies next to her head. Six cleats. It smells of mould, of swimming-pool changing cubicles and old clothes. His head pushes into her neck, he bites, he pulls up her blouse with his hands, the bra also, what is he doing, what is it? Hanna wants to call to him, say his name, it's suddenly become so different, he's hurting her, not like that, not like that. Not a sound comes from her mouth. He has put his arm across her throat and with his other hand he tugs down her panties. He pants, he talks, but she doesn't understand. Threads of spittle fall on her face. The agile hand burrows between her legs, the fingers worm in, and she feels a cutting pain as the sharp nails bore into her. Dirty nails with black rims, she saw them curved around the beer glass.

Extricate a leg, push off, bump with her knee between his legs. He loosens his grip. Hanna tears herself loose. "Goddammit. Ouch. What are you doing?" Jaak grabs his crotch. "You were asking for it, weren't you? To hell with you. Cow." He kicks open the door. In the frame of the doorpost she sees him smooth his hair with his hands.

It's very quiet in the locker room. Hanna sits with her arms around her knees. Her head is empty. She thinks about nothing. Stand up, pull up panties, tuck shirt into skirt, go outside.

Dee leans vomiting against the wall of the clubhouse. Kees stands next to her, his hands hanging by his sides. His face lights up when Hanna comes closer.

"She has to go home," he says. "She's had much too much beer." They place Dee between them and start on their way. Dee's legs drag over the ground. She leans heavily on her helpers and has to stop a few times along the way. "Party. We won. Have to puke." Hanna grips her friend tightly. In front of Deetje's house they stop.

"I'm going on," says Kees. "Tomorrow is Monday. Can you manage on your own?" Hanna nods. "Thank you. Bye." With her handkerchief she wipes trails of vomit from Dee's coat. Then she waves at Kees who, his hands in his pockets, quickly strides down the street. Up the step. Left arm behind Dee, ring with the right hand. Arnoud opens the door. "Here is Dee," says Hanna. "She's sick."

The house is dark. Hanna opens the garden gate and takes the kitchen-door key from under the rubbish bin. At the back of the garden the tops of the birches wave in the wind, leaves fall off, lit up by moonlight. No hunger ever again, thinks Hanna. I pick up my books, I carry my bag, my legs walk, and my mouth eats. I'll be someone who is never hungry. The lock clicks open. Hanna closes the door behind her.

Greek soccer

Like a flower in a pond, the island has grown up 41
to the water surface. We are going to live at the end of a
stalk that has sprouted from the bottom of the sea; between
boulders and rough waterplants it rose up month after
month. Now we come. Now come ships, laden with red
and white striped blankets and metal food bowls. Now
comes the work list, in Mr Morra's briefcase. My father's
name is on that list: Beuling, Pieter, dyke worker, Dutch
Reformed, married.

When Mr Morra crosses the narrow gang plank on
leaving the tugboat, he clasps the case against his chest with
his forearms. Then he stands on the ground, the new
ground, and looks around. Land is immediately land when

you set your feet on it. Stupid. Since I've been here, I dream that the stalk breaks and the island sinks into the sea. I feel that my bed tilts at an angle, my sister Kettie slides screaming out of the bed above me, I see her pajama legs fly through the air, her head bangs against the wall and I'm awake. Then I feel carefully in the space between the mattress and the side of the bed. My fingers caress the cardboard on which is the picture. The picture of Faas.

You can't just go and live on the island. You have to be assessed. I was still too small to understand any of it, but Kettie figured it out. She had to bring tea into the nice room where Mother sat on the velvet chairs with a strange woman. We'd had to put on our Sunday clothes; it was Tuesday, my blouse wasn't even dry yet and Mother stood puffing at the ironing board, her hair straggling over her eyes. "What a lot of nonsense for a woman like that," she mumbled. She combed me roughly, with water.

"We're going to move," Kettie whispered when she came back into the kitchen. "To a place where there's nothing. No school. Not even a street. She writes down everything about us. It's in the middle of the sea. She asked if I could swim." Kettie sniffed. Maybe she was lying, just for something to say. Before we came to the island, she always teased me.

Together with the other people who were approved we live in the barracks. Every family has a room with beds. I share the wardrobe with Kettie. Mother doesn't have to cook; Piet IJspeert in the canteen does that. When he's ready, he blows on a ship's horn and I go and get our food in a metal bowl. We sit on the lower beds with our plates on our laps. Very often Mother lies on my bed during the day. I hope she doesn't find the picture.

This is all about the fathers. We've just come along because we couldn't be left behind. The fathers are here for a purpose. The dredgers came first, to dig deep trenches far beneath the water with their dredging machines. Dripping, the buckets are pulled up and tipped over in the air. The dredgers never set foot on land, they sleep in their boats. On Saturdays, they all sail away, except for Wiebe's father; he lives in a houseboat called Beaver which is moored along-side our island. The dyke workers are the men who count. Every day they add another section on to the dykes which will one day connect us to the mainland. Now our island resembles a spider with ever longer legs, to Harderwijk, to Edam, to Vollenhove. Our fathers have to leave earlier and earlier to get to their section of dyke on time, and in the evening they come home later and later. Standing on the extreme tips of the spider legs, they seem to be out on the open sea. A squall, a swell, and they'll be thrashing about in the water. Work never stops. In the canteen, Mr Morra draws on his big map the sections that have been added during the day. At the top of the map is a diagonal stripe: the Barrier Dam. Ever since it's been there, the water has been called IJsselmeer, but everyone here still says Zuiderzee.

Especially the osier revetment workers. If they say anything at all. At the farthest end of the island they weave enormous mats from osiers which are then dragged to the newest section of dyke and are sunk with cartloads of rubble. The revetment workers wear flat black caps and don't associate with anyone. They live by themselves in the one wooden barracks that remained standing when the brick housing was built. They could live in the brick camp just like us, but they don't want to. Sometimes Arie and I steal up on them. In the dark of the morning they descend from the dyke, take a crap between the basalt blocks and wet their faces with water. We don't understand what they say to one another. They don't like the camp food. On Sunday evening, when they come on the tug from Vollenhove, they each have a pan of meat with them. They eat bits from that the whole week. They carry sharp knives to cut the stakes into a point and to peel their own potatoes.

At first I am always sad. There is nothing familiar: no ditch with tadpoles, no bridge, no soccer club. Not even a tree. I have nothing to do all day long. There are a few small children who walk around dressed in overalls. Kettie is always reading, and Mother rests on my bed. No flies against the windows. Always wind. Then Arie arrives. He wears rubber boots and has seen Faas Wilkes for real. Arie's parents get their own house; his father is a barber and his mother sells beauty products. Arie has swiped a lipstick from her to give to Kettie. Nonchalantly my sister lets the present slide into her pocket. But then again she has no lips to speak of.

He gives me the picture; I may keep it. I wish I had a sweater like that with stripes, a Xerxes team sweater like Faas is wearing. I look in the small mirror that hangs on the wall between the beds and slick back my hair with a wet comb so that it looks dark, almost as black as Faas's hair. I look at myself, a little from below, my head slightly bent. With pitch-black eyes, I look like him.

Arie and I fish with fishing-poles we make ourselves. We hunt for rats; we use bread crusts to lure the animals up onto the dyke and then pelt them mercilessly with stone bullets from a catapult. Behind the revetment workers' barracks, a stick has begun to sprout. Now there is a tree on the island.

Arie turns eleven and his parents give him a soccer ball, a real sewn-up one. In front of their house he is keeping the ball in the air, three short kicks and the ball bounces away, two headers, and Arie falls down. "Get away from there," says his mother, "next you'll break my windows. Off with you." We try kicking on the dyke which suddenly seems very narrow. I kick the ball into the water right through Arie's legs. We can catch it, thanks to the wind. Now the ball is really heavy, as if you're kicking against a

45

basalt block. Sometimes we play a short match against Wiebe and his brother Gijs, on the grass near the canteen. Piet IJspeert comes outside with a pan filled with potatoes which he strains in the drain next to the door. He shakes his head amidst the clouds of steam and points to the windows of the barracks surrounding the field. "It's not allowed here either," says Wiebe. He wants to grab the ball, but I kick it straight to Arie. It drives right past helpless Gijs. The canteen door groans. Five-nothing.

Autumn comes, and Mr Morra has said that we should have classes. Because there is no school on the island, he has appealed to my mother. He's sitting in the canteen with her; he has placed his hat on the table while keeping his coat on. Piet is doing dishes and has pushed the kitchen partition open so that he can hear what is being discussed. I had walked along with Mother, with the flashlight.

"That wind," she says, "always that lousy wind, it blows your ears off your head."

I dry the serving spoons and the enormous knives for Piet. Through the partition I hear Mr Morra's high voice. He talks about idleness and vandalism.

"Discipline, Mrs Beuling, and a worthwhile way to spend the day. You have experience."

"I have only done it with pre-schoolers," says Mother, "and that was long ago. And I'm always tired here." "That's because you have nothing to do. The cooking is done for you, you have hardly any housework to do. The government agency does all that for you. Now you can do something for the Rijksdienst!"

She has no choice. Every morning from eight-thirty until twelve-thirty she stands in front of what is supposed to be a class: twelve or so children, of whom Kettie at thirteen is the oldest and the ever-sniffling Stibbe twins, who have just turned four, are the youngest. We sit at tables in the canteen where it smells of stale coffee and stubbed-out cigars. Piet is poking around in the kitchen. He has made a low table out of packing crates, with benches of rough wood for the smallest children. One of the twins gets a splinter in his thigh and cries softly. It's cold but not yet time for the heater. I sit at a table with Arie, Wiebe and Gijs; we're drawing on paper from Mr Morra, which has been typed on one side. "Teacher, they have snotty noses," says Geertje Stibbe as she points at the twins with her thumb. Mother looks around the room, takes a dish towel from the bar and blows the twins' noses. Exhausted, she sits down in a chair that's too low. She doesn't wear an apron. Her skirt has been fastened around her waist with a safety pin. She brushes the hair from her face and sighs. I look out of the window and see grey water.

Mother is unable to develop a reading programme that satisfies everyone. The little ones want to sing songs for hours on end every day, the bigger boys don't feel like it. Arie pinches Wiebe's bottom unexpectedly, causing him to yell out; Kettie helps the twins in the toilet and returns

47

with her mouth painted scarlet. Mother looks alternately at Kettie and at the fighting boys. I concentrate on my drawing.

Geography, Mr Morra has said. Mother had to talk about the sea and our special position in it. And our history. She can certainly talk about the war as she experienced it, that was such a short time ago. She starts with the bombardment of Rotterdam, meanwhile Arie draws airplanes with black swastikas on them and the little ones look at her surprised. They become afraid. I think of the destroyed streets and squares in Faas's city. Maybe he's walking around there just as uprooted as I am on this island, across chaotic expanses where nothing yet exists, past excavations and fences behind which things will eventually rise, across sandy ground with stones and pieces of wood, while the wind blows raindrops against his face.

"He's playing in Italy, he's sitting nice and comfortably in the sun on a terrace," says Arie. But I draw him in a Xerxes-team uniform. Myself too, for that matter. I am a very young but very good left wing and feed him good shots all of which Faas pops in. "Thanks," he says. The goalkeeper stands crying in the goal.

Arithmetic books have come from Volendam, and Mother is trying to explain long division to the big kids. I listen but I hear nothing, only the tired sound of her voice.

"Carry, add, borrow, don't forget the decimal . . . How was that supposed to be done again, do you know, Kettie?" Kettie looks up from her book and shakes her head.

The school in Vollenhove has donated an unmarked map of Holland. Piet IJspeert hangs it behind the bar and starts competing with Mother in identifying the names of cities and rivers. The Zuiderzee is still open. In its centre there is nothing, no island, no dot, nothing.

Yet we exist, on the artificial island that is officially called *Parcel P*. The tugboats from Enkhuizen, Harderwijk and Vollenhove can usually manage to find us to deliver supplies and mail. Janus Blom, Arie's father, sorts the letters in his barbershop and then brings them around wearing his postman's cap. Mother says he reads them first.

It freezes; the sea freezes over. Not one boat can get through. Is there enough coal on the island for the large heaters in the barracks? Piet burns loose wood in the canteen heater; it sputters and crackles, making the children restless. Once a week a helicopter comes; it hangs suspended over the dyke and then burlap bags containing packages, papers, clothes and food rain down. The bags tear, letters blow in between the basalt blocks, and oranges roll down the dykes. We crawl over the rocks and gather up everything.

Even though it's forbidden, we play between the ice piling up on the dyke, in creaking, cold castles. The houseboat of Wiebe's parents disappears behind the slabs of ice. The whole island crunches and creaks. Mrs Stibbe is about to have a baby but can't reach the mainland. Mr Morra is stuck in Enkhuizen, and Mother closes the school. A day off to go skating, she says. She's going to help Mrs Stibbe and deposits the twins with Kettie.

When Father comes back from work, Mother isn't back yet; Kettie stations herself under the window to listen to the screaming. "Fly a doctor over," says Father, "or at least connect a telephone, couldn't the government at least do that for us?" He mashes the beans on his tin plate. The windows shake in their frames. Storm. I think of Faas on his Italian terrace. He feeds the pigeons and from under his dark eyebrows he looks at the dazzling sky.

Mother stays in bed the next day. The baby was stillborn, says Kettie. Lots of blood, and Mrs Stibbe doesn't even want to see the twins. The storm continues, even at night.

Mr Morra manages to get himself transported to the island in between the melting ice floes. Arie and I are standing by the tugboat when it goes back with Mrs Stibbe on board. Her face is hidden in a heavy shawl. The captain carries a box inside. The baby, thinks Arie. It could also be cigars. The boat pounds incessantly against the landing piles, and there are white crests on the water.

A switchboard has been installed. Arie's mother Agnes learns how to operate it; their house has the most space and Arie's father is already taking care of the mail. It's as if they can reach farther than all of us. From the hair salon Agnes can call the hospital in Harderwijk and the office in Enkhuizen. I call up Faas, every night. He dribbles ahead of me with the ball, and I imitate him. Turn, cut, around the ball, kick low on the ball, shoot. He turns around and gives a thumbs-up sign. His black hair is plastered impeccably against his head, for where we are there is no wind.

Agnes Blom comes pounding on all the barracks doors. "Flooding," she says with her perfectly painted mouth. "Storm tide in Zeeland. The men have to go there." With both hands she holds onto her hairdo, as though her hair would otherwise blow from her head. The door of the barracks bangs shut when she strides off with her skinny hips.

It's true. All the fathers trudge on to the tugboat which comes chugging in from Harderwijk very early in the morning. Wiebe and Gijs see Mr Wagenvoort off. Mr Stibbe comes to the landing alone. Janus may stay on the island, and Piet too. Father kisses all of us. When he came back last night from the discussion with Mr Morra, he told us what it's like in Zeeland: people are sitting on the roofs of their houses and waving white pillowcases, boats are sailing around between steeples and chimneys, drowned pigs are bobbing on the waves, and the sea is sweeping through the broken dykes. It goes without saying that Father has to go there. I run to the end of the dyke with Arie. We wave at the tugboat until we can't see it any more.

51

Barely a week after the fathers have left, the boat from Enkhuizen arrives with a new island inhabitant. In his high rubber boots he is down the gangplank in three steps. Brown corduroy trousers. A duffel coat with anchor buttons. A pointed face; black, combed back, wavy hair. I feel a tugging in my stomach. Mr Morra dribbles behind the man. Both of them walk towards the group of waiting mothers and children. "Schoolmaster Greidanus," says Morra. "He has come to instruct you from now on. Thanks to the government." The teacher is rocking back and forth on his feet; he stretches his back and looks over the whole island. Then his glance lowers slowly to the level of the mothers' faces. Agnes Blom smiles. Mother scowls. The master's glance drops lower and inspects the children. Kettie has her hands at her back. She sticks her chin up in the wind and looks at the teacher until he turns his eyes to Arie and me. I stand up straighter. Furtively, Arie pokes me in the back. The teacher sees it. He says nothing. He looks calmly at the small children and nods at Geertje who holds a twin with each hand. She blushes.

"I expect you tomorrow morning. The big kids at eight-thirty, the kindergartners at nine. In the temporary school building." His voice sounds loud, maybe he's afraid he won't be heard through the wind. He turns around and goes to collect his suitcase from the dock.

Now we're a real school. The teacher has put our chairs behind the tables so that we all look straight ahead at him.

He has shut the partition to the kitchen. It's quiet in the classroom. Each child works at his own assignments. You're never allowed to do nothing. When you finish an assignment you have to come forward. You stand by the teacher's table while he reads your exercise book. Then he looks at you and in a restrained voice he tells you what mistakes you've made. Schoolmaster Greidanus does not bother with the pre-schoolers. He had their small-sized furniture moved to the scullery.

At nine o'clock on the first day of school, Mother came to look after the little ones and saw the children sitting wedged between buckets and brooms. There was an argument. Mr Morra had to step in. Mother was dismissed and Agnes Blom volunteered to succeed her.

At lunchtime Agnes discusses the lesson programme with the teacher. In the afternoon, we, the older ones, also have school. We push the tables to the sides and have gym class. The teacher had all the mothers sew black shorts. My mother thought it was nonsense. I put on my father's old swimming trunks, and Kettie gets shorts from Geertje that are too tight around her bottom.

53

We have to steel ourselves, says the teacher. We should imagine that we live in a valley. Everywhere around us there are mountains; behind them lives the enemy. That's why we have to become watchful, united and strong. Just like the old Greeks the teacher tells us about. They were willing to sacrifice everything for their country; they would run a race and wrestle in their bare skin while it was freezing. I wrestle with Arie in front of the heater. I sit on top of him and teacher watches. "You're breaking his strength," he says. "That's how you get to know each other. As soldiers, as brothers." We of the new land can only trust one another. The old land is rotten. Those from the old land are our enemies.

Sometimes the fathers come home on Saturday evening, leaving again early Monday morning. All the dykes in Zeeland are destroyed, the best dyke workers from all over Holland will have to work on the repairs for a long time. The old land is falling apart, it's worn out. Mr Morra wants to invite a class from Biggekerke to let them recover on our island. He talked about it with the teacher, Agnes says to Mother. "But Evert doesn't care for that at all, he's already working much too hard."

"It doesn't seem so great for those children," says Mother, "they've already seen much too much water."

"But the ones from Vollenhove or Nijkerk," I say to Arie, "can't they come? There's enough space for them to stay now the men are gone. We can have a game."

Arie goes to teacher Greidanus. The soldiers of the new land want to fight their enemies. We're going to train. Piet places woven iron mats against the windows at the back of the barracks; when the pre-schoolers want to play outside, they have to go to the field in front of the canteen, and we have the inside fields for practice.

Teacher calls the girls boys. We need them badly for the team, and Kettie is a great goalkeeper. Every afternoon we have to practise trapping, tackling, passing and shooting. Geertje turns out to be terrific at heading. After dinner we have to line up for a practice match, five against five. We have to feed the ball to each other, let each other score; we have to be a unit, says teacher. Arie calls it Greek soccer. Mother grumbles to herself as we leave in our black shorts.

"He no longer sleeps," says Agnes Blom, "and look at his eyes glitter. That man is just burning up." For weeks the teacher has been talking about nothing but the match against the old land. We should all sleep together, he feels, no longer near our mothers. And then in the morning, go naked into the cold sea. That's what makes you a unit. Arie titters and nudges Kettie. "Don't look at me," she says.

Teacher tells how we have to humiliate those from Nijkerk; mercilessly we have to show them which team is the healthiest, the friendliest, the strongest. He speaks loud and fast. At times spittle flies out of his mouth. If only the dykes in Zeeland were finished.

On the stick tree there are buds that get fatter by the day. The tree is alive. Arie and I play soccer on the dyke. We can aim so well that the ball no longer falls into the water. It's still early. Behind the empty revetment workers' shed we hear thumping. We creep closer and see the teacher standing naked on the basalt blocks. He lifts his arms. His enormous dick swings back and forth. Then the teacher is swimming. He sees us and raises an arm to lure us into the water. Arie goes, but keeps his underpants on. I watch for a minute, then I run away.

The boat with the Nijkerk group is approaching. We stand on the landing, in soccer clothing, to welcome the enemy. Mrs Wagenvoort and Agnes have baked cakes for the reception in the canteen. Janus Blom stands in the back. He'll be referee this afternoon. We have to show the Nijkerk group around the island so that they can see how we live here. There are many of them, many more than the eleven that are needed. They stumble over the stones of the dyke, they hurt their bare knees on the wood scraps that have washed ashore everywhere. They keep going on that we don't have real houses, that nothing grows here, that there isn't even a church. I consider showing them the stick tree, but I don't.

Piet has built two real goals, using discarded fishnets. The Nijkerk team comes onto the field. They don't want to play against girls, but when they see the teacher, they restrain themselves and line up. They all look like they're fourteen years old. Kettie positions herself in her goal and spits into her hands.

Before we came outside, we all stood in the scullery, bent over, with our arms around each other. Geertje Stibbe's cheek against mine. Hissing, teacher whispered that we were special, a new kind of person from a new land. It wasn't important that we had to go onto the field minus one man. Unity was our eleventh man.

I'm the captain, and I shake hands with the enemy who steps forward in real cleats. From the sideline teacher looks at me scornfully; I wipe my hand on my shorts. Meanwhile the ball is already gone. Wiebe Wagenvoort trots back and forth like a horse in front of Kettie's goal. Nevertheless: a goal. They start to cheer. "Take your positions! Keep playing!" roars teacher. The cheering dies down. Panting and with his whistle at the ready, Janus Blom crosses the field. The mothers call out softly: "Let's go, let's go." The small children are silent.

During half-time Nijkerk retreats to the revetment workers' shed, their locker room. Piet brings them tea. Through the canteen window I see Agnes walking behind the teacher; her red mouth moves fast. Teacher waves his arms though the air as if he wants to sweep her away. "I want to get going," says Janus, "at least it will be over. Give me a carnival any time." Teacher storms into the canteen. "In war all weapons are permitted," he says. "The new land doesn't lose. Exterminate them! Wipe them out at any price.

Better death than defeat, remember that!" He looks pale. I give a sign to my team of only ten. We go outside.

We have the wind at our backs. Geertje gets the ball on her head and heads it in. "Offside," says Janus. From the sideline the teacher roars that Janus is blind, doesn't know the rules, doesn't know where he is. "The referee is impartial, Mr Greidanus," says Janus. Tough and straight-backed, teacher walks to the end of the field. Arie has the ball. I run so that I'm open, the ball comes and with one movement I kick it into the goal. In a mist of sweat and tears I see Faas standing by Kettie's goal. His wavy hair. The smile on his thin lips. Now it's war. Even the girls kick the shins of the Nijkerk team. When their centre forward tries to score, little Gijs Wagenvoort drags him down by pulling on his pants. Indignant, the Nijkerkers shout at Janus who lets the play continue. Closing ranks we swarm forward, we can, we can.

"Fire!" screams Kettie. She is jumping up and down between the goalposts and points at the shed behind her. A window shatters into fragments and thick clouds of smoke come out. Flames flare up immediately. There's rustling, there's crackling. Paralysed, the players stand on the grass. Janus gives three very short whistles. Still no one moves. Everyone listens to the hissing of the burning revetment workers shed.

Piet comes rushing up with buckets. "Put it out," he says, "plenty of water. Go and stand in a line. Pass them on. I'll fling them in."

The Nijkerkers start shouting for their shoes, their coats, their backpacks and their spending money. "Shut up and help," says Piet. Agnes Blom storms straight through the fire-fighting line. "Evert, where is Evert? Evert is burning!" Piet gets ready to tear the stick out of the ground in order to batter in the door with it. Shall I go and defend my tree or will it then be my fault if teacher dies? The door opens by itself and a smoking shape rushes out. With big steps he runs to the sea. Showers of sparks splash against the basalt; sizzling, the teacher goes under. His hairs float in the water. I have soot in my eyes; they sting.

The tugboat comes to pick up the children from Nijkerk. Without a word they climb into the boat, one after the other, shivering in their dirty soccer clothes. The captain is about to lift the ship's horn to announce the departure when three figures walk slowly to the gang plank. Mother and Piet IJspeert support the teacher between them. He is wrapped in a red and white blanket; around it two straps are pulled so tightly that he can barely move. He walks on bare feet, like the old Greeks, says Arie. Teacher keeps on whispering: "Destroy. Start over. The solution is fire." Yellow-white blobs cake the corners of his mouth.

Mother helps him to go with Piet into the back of the pilot house, far from the hold. The boat leaves for Harderwijk where the parents of the Nijkerk children are waiting at the harbor, where the captain and Piet bring teacher to the hospital, where the land is old.

"Agnes didn't make any sense," says Mother. "She was just panting into the telephone, and to a doctor at that. I took the phone away from her. They know that he's coming. Go and sleep, it's over."

I hear Kettie breathing above me. I don't close my eyes. Water and fire. I grope in the space next to the mattress and take out the picture of Faas. My muscles ache. Arie, Geertje, Wiebe, Gijs, Kettie—we all lie on this island without streets or churches, an island that stretches its tentacles to all sides to find something to hold onto, the island that gently rocks back and forth on the waves. I press the photo against my chest with both hands. Water. Fire.

The artificial island of Lelystad actually existed; the persons, circumstances and events described are imaginary.

Sweets

Nora van der Mare wakes up but doesn't move
yet. She listens to the rasping breathing of her little brother
Hein. Hein's bed stands on the other side of the room;
Nora can't see him. She always sleeps with her face turned
to her own wall.

What was going on? What was it? Papa. Nora gets a
strange feeling in her stomach. Papa was in Australia, for a
whole year. He doesn't know that Hein's hair has been cut,
that Mummy has a new shiny blue bathrobe. And he doesn't
know that I have turned eleven. Now he is back, but not
really.

Nora sits up. Hein's mouth hangs open and he holds

his fists clenched under his chin. Hein has very thin arms, like sticks. He's only eight.

In the bathroom, Nora brushes her hair with Mummy's brush. That's forbidden.

I want thick, black hair, not such a mousy colour. I got that from Papa. Why didn't Mummy give me her hair? Then it would curl. Perhaps they would have called me Ellie. Or Mia. Nora is so stupid.

Van der Mare is even more stupid. The boys start to whinny when I pass. Later I can get married to someone who has a normal name. To Walter, then I'll be called Meier, just like Els. Does Walter want to marry a girl whose name is Mare?

The skirt with the three flounces has an ugly spot right in the front. Nora puts it on. It's too tight; with difficulty she twists the skirt over her hips so that the spot is at the back. Where the upper flounce borders the middle one, the seam cuts into her thighs. Her sweater is also tight and has moved when she tugged the skirt round. The knitted cables stretch over her nipples. Breasts! If she has to run, they shake back and forth, and she crosses her arms in front of them. Els runs much faster, she's still quite flat.

Nora takes a large sweater from the winter wardrobe and goes downstairs.

Halfway down the stairs you can look into the living

room through a wide indoor window that was installed in the hallway. The room is empty. That means Mummy is in the kitchen.

She is wearing her new robe. Silver feathers are painted on the deep blue. Mummy has tanned legs with thin ankles. Her toenails are painted pink. She stands by the stove, stirring a small pan. She pours oatmeal into a bowl that she puts on the kitchen table in front of Nora. Nora puts a pat of butter in the oatmeal and sprinkles brown sugar over it. Mummy sits down at the other side of the table; she leans her back against the wall and lights a cigarette. The smoke smells good.

"Why isn't Papa here?"

"He is here. He's in the hospital. Now eat, otherwise you'll be late."

"Is he sick?"

"The doctors have to figure that out. He's in quarantine."

"What's that?"

"No one can be with him. Only the doctors."

"Haven't you seen him either?"

"No. Now eat!"

Nora spoons up the oatmeal. The sugar has melted and makes dark brown trails in the oatmeal. It reminds Nora of Hein's dirty pants. He can't hold back his poo. He folds up the pants and hides them at the bottom of the laundry basket. It's an illness, says Mummy. That's why Hein almost never has to go to school.

"May I have a bra?"

Nora's mother looks up and bursts out laughing. "How old are you anyway? You really don't need it. Half the time I don't wear the thing either. If you'd stand up straight, you'd see for yourself. Els doesn't have a bra either, does she? She keeps her back straight."

The laugh has disappeared from Mummy's face. That happens very fast. She laughs—and right away her face is completely expressionless again.

"Finish your plate. I don't stand here cooking for no good reason at this hour."

Nora stands up. She puts the half-empty plate in the sink.

"You're too fat, that's it. That skirt is much too tight, disgusting. Why are you so fat, that doesn't look cute, you know!"

Quarantine, quarantine, thinks Nora. Papa is in quarantine. It seems like a land from a fairy tale and yet it is here, in the big hospital behind the station. I won't ask if Hein has to go to school. I might have to take him with me. Then he'll start screaming or run away, back home. Hein isn't fat, he's just as thin as Mummy.

Nora puts on the heavy sweater.

"For goodness sake, that's much too warm. You'll sweat and stink. Take it off!"

Nora walks around the table to give Mummy a kiss. From the robe comes a glorious scent; it comes from the large bottle which says Worth.

A kiss on Nora's cheek. A slender tanned hand on the mousy hair.

"Bye my girl, see you later."

Across the street Els is waiting in a sleeveless summer dress. She has a schoolbag with handles which she can carry on her back. Her straight back.

Along the waterway buttercups and sorrel stand mixed together. You can smell that it's going to be a warm day.

"I'll ask my father if we can go to the beach tonight," says Els. "He says it's too cold to go swimming, but we could at least go there. Do you want to come?"

"If I can."

Nora bounces the bag alternately against the front and the back of her legs. Chubby, fat, she thinks, quarantine, quarantine.

In class she keeps on her sweater. When it's recess, she doesn't go outside. With her last pocket money she buys a gingerbread from the janitor. The cakes lie in big, square boxes. Nora wants one with pink icing on it. Slowly she walks to the book corner where the encyclopedia stands. It begins with a Q. It's a hygienic measure, to safeguard public health. The patient is isolated for forty days. Forty days, that's more than a month! By then it'll be summer, it'll be vacation. The patient has cholera or tuberculosis. That can't be Papa. We would know that.

Nora shuts the book. The gingerbread is finished but

she is still hungry. Her stomach feels strange, maybe it's not hunger but a stomach ache, like Hein's.

Teacher says that the school doctor has come today. One by one, all the children have to see her, for the last time at elementary school.

"She looks in the boys' pants," whispers Els, "she squeezes their balls. Walter told me!"

Doctor Bording sits in the principal's office. She has a grey and black bun and wears glasses. She asks how Nora's mother is doing.

"It's not easy to have so many illnesses at home. It's a good thing you're so big already. Do you help a lot? And now you're going to high school, almost. Lift up your sweater for a moment so that I can listen to your lungs."

Nora has to sigh, and the doctor puts the cold circle of the stethoscope on various places against her back.

She's a doctor, thinks Nora; shall I ask her about quarantine? And about breasts?

"Have you had your big M yet?" Doctor Bording asks suddenly.

Nora pulls her sweater down. She can't manage to tuck it into the waistband. Then just leave it out.

"Have you had your period yet?"

Nora blushes. She shakes her head. No.

"Then it will happen very soon, I think." The doctor looks at Nora's upper body. "You're a big healthy girl. Give

my regards to your mother. Tell her that I'll call her soon
to talk about your brother."

Doctor Bording bends her head to write something
on a chart. The bun sticks up. Nora wants to say something,
but her throat is so dry that the words stick. Silently she
leaves the office.

Mummy is reading in the garden. The bathrobe hangs completely open. Mummy has small breasts, tanned from the
sun, as tanned as her face and her feet.

"Are you back already? I didn't know that it was so
late! I have to go to the doctor with Hein this afternoon.
You'll have to do the shopping. Three small steaks and two
litres of milk. I've put ten guilders on the table. Will you
make yourself a sandwich?"

When they are gone, Nora takes bread, butter, and
the tin with chocolate sprinkles. She pushes the lid of the
tin down hard onto the thickly spread slice of bread. A
sweet treat of bread and chocolate. She spreads butter on
the left-over crusts. She dips them into the tin and in this
way makes sweet croquettes.

In the shopping street Nora looks at the paving stones.
People will think that she's a girl remembering which
errands she has to do for her mother. The ten guilder bill
is in the front pocket of the school bag.

The flower shop smells of perfume and water.

"I want to send a bouquet to the hospital," says Nora.

The lady walks past all the buckets with her, and Nora points out which flowers she wants to have in the bouquet. Big flowers with long stems, peonies, lilies, and stocks. The lady arranges them and ties a string around the bouquet. Nora sighs. It looks beautiful.

She has to write the address on a piece of paper: Mr van der Mare, Hospital, Quarantine Ward.

"And now a card for the bouquet," says the lady. She places a small white piece of cardboard with gold edges in front of Nora. It's warm in the store; the sweater itches Nora's back. She waits until she has thought of something. Nothings comes to her. With big letters she writes NORA in the center of the card.

68

One guilder is left, just enough for a giant bag of frosted cremes. On the soft-yellow and pink icing there is a powder-like layer which melts against your tongue. It's not until then that the sweet taste comes out and you can press your teeth through the spongy sweet. It slides down your throat like a caress.

"I lost it. Vanished. It wasn't there any more when I got to the butcher's."

"I can't leave anything to you! You don't pay attention, you don't think. Lost ten guilders, how did you manage to do it?"

Because I'm stupid, thinks Nora. Stupid and fat. I'm so fat that I feel nothing, the bank notes blow from between my fingers and I don't feel it. It happens and I've already forgotten it.

"Just go to your room. And take your stuff with you."

Mummy stamps her foot and with her arm extended she points to the door.

Nora puts her sweater and school bag on the stairs. Quickly she walks upstairs. There she lies down on her bed. She pulls the pillow over her head.

"Nora, Nora, we're leaving!"

Els stands under the window, her head back as she looks up at Nora.

"I'm sure I won't be allowed to go. My mother's mad at me."

"Why?"

"I lost the money for the errands."

Nora leans over the windowsill. The window frame presses against her breasts. Pain, pain and itch.

"Just go and ask. I'll wait."

In the living room Mummy and Hein are playing Junior Scrabble. Hein lines up his small blocks with letters. He swings his skinny legs under his chair. A stack of newspapers lies on the table, Nora reads upside-down:

NUCLEAR BLAST IN WESTERN AUSTRALIA

That's an explosion. Perhaps a volcano. Good that Papa left there in time.

"You may go," says Mummy. "Mr Meier already mentioned it; we ran into him in town. Take along a towel!"

Mummy and Hein's heads bend towards each other. Which letter will they use? Their necks show that they belong together. Both have a double mound with a downy groove in between.

The twins sit in the front next to Mr Meier. Nora, Els and Walter slide into the back seat. The car roof is open; warm wind blows the hair out of Nora's face.

"Are we going to sing, Papa?" asks Els.

"Yes, a round," says Mr Meier. "Just start, then I'll come in."

They do "Frère Jacques", and then the song of the big and small clocks. Els and Walter get confused and can't hold their parts. Els sings along with Nora and Walter, with his father.

"I'll teach you 'White Coral Bells'," says Mr Meier, "that's so beautiful."

First they sing the song together. Then Mr Meier starts, with the twins. Els and Walter take the second part; Nora pokes Els in the ribs when they have to come in. Finally Nora joins in. She listens to the deep voice of Mr Meier and twines her song around it. The others have fallen silent.

"I'd always want to sing with you, Noortje, you do it so beautifully!" Mr Meier turns around and smiles. Nora smiles back.

There are hard ridges in the sand. Between them shells lie in small puddles of water. The sea pushes an edge of foam across the beach. The water is cold but the sand is still warm. Mr Meier has also taken off his shoes and socks. He has rolled up his trousers. Nora sees a carpet of black hair on his shins.

He puts his hand on her neck and squeezes gently. "It's not easy. For your mother it's all very difficult, you know that. Your mother is a very brave woman."

Nora stands still with her feet in the water. The sea pulls the sand from under her, it tickles, she sinks. Then she runs away, to the others.

"Hungry, Papa, we're hungry!"

The twin sisters hang on Mr Meier's coat. He goes to a store on the boulevard with Walter, and the girls have to choose a beautiful spot for the picnic. On a dune.

Walter carries a bottle of buttermilk. Mr Meier hands out double slices of bread with a slice of pink ham in between. Everyone gets a tomato.

What special food, thinks Nora. It tastes so strong, more delicious than anything I've ever tasted.

"Come here, Noortje." With his pocket knife Mr Meier cuts slices from a cucumber, and Nora places them between her bread slices. She eats slowly. The sun has become a large red ball. They sit next to one another with their faces turned to the sea, they pass the bottle and see the sun slowly disappear in the water.

Carefully Nora walks to her bed in the dark room. She doesn't turn on the light because Hein is already asleep. Mummy smiled when she came home and asked if she still wanted to eat anything. She was wearing the dress with a hundred buttons. She had put on lipstick and had pinned a flower from the garden on her dress. The newspapers were no longer on the table.

Nora slides in between the sheets and falls asleep at once.

When she wakes up she thinks that she's heard something: a door banging shut, a bell? She sits up. It is quiet. Now Nora notices that her stomach hurts. She flings her arms around herself and rocks back and forth. It doesn't go away.

On the toilet she is alarmed: in her underpants there is an elongated brown-red spot. Hein's illness. Now there's no one healthy in the house. Nora puts her head between her knees. The spot doesn't smell of poo at all, but of iron and salt.

Nora feels that she has to cry and blinks her eyelids hard to hold back her tears. She pulls up her pants and goes downstairs.

Through the hall window she sees the yellowish light of the floor lamp. Mummy sits on the sofa and Mr Meier sits next to her. The door of the room stands open but here, in the hall, it's dark. Nora sits down on the stairs, next to her school bag.

Mr Meier has put his arms around Mummy and presses her head against his shirt. He caresses her face. She's crying. "Pet, my little pet," says Mr Meier.

Around Nora the air is icy cold. There is a lump in her school bag, her hand slips in and finds the bag with frosted cremes. One after the other she sticks them into her mouth and eats them without thinking. There is only the movement from bag to mouth; from lips to throat. For the rest everything stands still.

Mummy has her eyes closed and her hands in Mr Meier's hair. He has unbuttoned the dress; he is kneeling next to the sofa and kisses the small, tanned breasts.

Nora watches and eats, eats, eats.

"Where a lord washes his hands"

To Dr E. Kallander

Chief Curator of the Cabinet of the Golden Age in The Hague

Dear Dr Kallander,
  My name is Helena Lievaert.

Why should he care about that? What else? Although I'm forty years old I still look good: the right proportions, fine colouring, good figure. Healthy too, and not stupid.

I am writing to you to tell you about an experience and to ask your advice.

Experience? Stupid word. Scratch it. Start again.

Last week I was in Delft, and something happened to me there that I would like to tell you about.

Delft? What was I doing in Delft? Should he know that? Better tell him so that he won't think that I'm just someone off the street.

I was invited there to read at an architecture conference. The final event took place in the City Hall on Grote Markt.

This letter is getting too long. I'll lose his attention. I say too much and much too little. He should know that the most important architects in the world were sitting in the auditorium. The highest-ranking officials. Ministers, presidents of international companies. The mayor, the royal commissioner, the crown prince.

And Leentje Lievaert, the daughter of the milkman. I come from an inherently contradictory family. My mother was a countess, my father put pencil marks in a school notebook to count the bottles of buttermilk that he sold daily. She had run away, my mother, run away with that black-haired, fiery boy who played the accordion with his bony fingers. She broke with her family and renounced all her rights. I inherited my fortune later from a headstrong aunt. Growing up in the rooms behind the store was quite the opposite of fortunate. I liked helping my father to arrange bottles in the refrigerated display case, but Mother looked cross when I jumped up to go to the front. She gave me books to read and let me do my homework quietly at the table in the square kitchen. I liked that too, but Father sniffed disdainfully when he walked past me to wash his hands in the sink. A hidden rift, a shaky balance.

They are both dead, they lie buried next to each other.

I stood on that magnificent marble floor and read my series of poems about Vermeer. On a table at the back of the hall, the bookseller had arranged all my books to suit the occasion: the essays about landscape and urban development, the treatise on colours and the volumes of poetry. The men listened, sunk in the antique seats. I wore a milkmaid-blue coat.

I digress. What I write sounds simple, as if it happened just like that, but I was in Delft, after more than twenty years I was back in Delft and I opened my mouth. I didn't fall down, I didn't start to scream, nor did I flee. I spoke quietly and they listened.

That is not without significance, Mr Kallander. Delft is the most disagreeable city on earth, and the most dissatisfied and foul-tempered people are to be found there. They have a view of the most picturesque buildings, and the scent of water rises into their noses when they walk along the canals, but they complain about the narrow paving-stones and swear at the drizzle. In Delft nothing's ever good.

At school I was alone. The teacher read my papers with a certain respect; behind my back the pupils rattled their coins so that I would not forget that while we were in class my father pushed his milk cart past their houses, opened doors by pulling on the rope that hung outside the mail slots, placed the milk in the hall and took the coins out of the metal milk tin. I didn't know how I was supposed to behave, so I didn't behave. I couldn't figure out where I belonged, so I belonged nowhere. For the first seventeen years of my life I had only one thought: get away!

I have to think of Kallander. I have to give a business-like and succinct report of the event, on a new sheet of paper.

Dear Mr Kallander,

You are the greatest Vermeer expert in Holland. This is why I am addressing my question to you.

Harry held a letter in front of me.

"Shouldn't you reply to this? They're offering five thousand guilders."

Harry is my agent. He sorts my mail, makes appointments for interviews and appearances, and organizes my finances. He is bald, still has a few dark curls on his broad neck and peers innocently through round glasses. He negotiates with my publisher like a shrewd market vendor: quickly, pleasantly, successfully. Every week he sits in my study for a whole morning and organizes my life. He has a mother. What else he does I don't know. I don't imagine him amidst wife and children, rather, I see him late at night at the door of a private gay bar in The Hague. I never ask.

"Delft," I said. "Do you know what a really scary city that is? I'm not going there."

"Yes, you are. You'll dress up nicely and I'll drive you there. Read, answer questions, sign, then a glass of wine with the directors and whoosh, on the freeway. Back home before twelve. Everyone satisfied."

What was I so scared of? That the citizens of Delft would stand around me like a grey wall, that my words would bounce off their smooth skulls, that they would turn away from me sneering, rattling the coins in their trouser pockets? I have been so unhappy in that city, so out of place, so desperate.

79

Of course I fell in love. Someone would have to save me. Not my classmates. I went to no one's home, I didn't give parties when I had a birthday because I didn't dare to invite anyone to our milk palace. Perhaps they thought I was arrogant, standoffish and conceited. My skin was like a pale peach because of the excessive milk consumption. I walked erect, as if I were forever going to my execution. I had my mother make black clothes for me long before it became fashionable.

On Wednesday afternoons they would bicycle to the hockey field; when there was a fair on the Markt they wandered squealing past the merry-go-rounds and the cotton candy booths; in the summer they attacked one another in the turbid water of the outdoor pool. I helped my father with the bookkeeping, took long walks in the polders, to Abtswoude, to Pijnacker. I read.

It was a teacher. Still a child, now that I think about it. At twenty-five he came as a substitute for our Dutch teacher when the latter succumbed to alcohol. He paid no attention to the pestering that tested him; it seemed as if his love for literature made him invulnerable. Roland Holst he read with us, Achterberg, Lucebert. He led me to understand poetry, even when it was hard to understand. He showed how you could go into the poem, how you could savour every word, how the insights at each word could help you on your way even if the word itself offered no solution, how everything had a function within the world of that one page.

"There is often one more than I count," he read and looked at me. In the back of the class my hands shook holding the thin volume. He knows, I thought, he understands. I am that one.

In the afternoon he walked to the station to take the train to Amsterdam. The book bag hung on his left side, I walked at his right. He talked: about the essays he had us write, about the magic power of words, about the light of Delft. I didn't say much, but at the right moments I looked at his face and he saw that I understood him. On my birthday he gave me a reproduction of *The Music Lesson* by Vermeer. I was the silent young woman at the harpsichord; he, the infatuated young man who watched her. A domineering creep, I thought, but I stuck the picture above my bed because I had never seen the oppressive atmosphere of Delft portrayed so strikingly.

He took me with him to The Hague; to my parents I said it was a compulsory museum visit with the school. We saw the *View of Delft*, and for the first time in my life I cried on seeing a painting. I remained sitting on the round bench in front of it for at least an hour and with my eyes I took in the canvas, from left to right, from bottom to top.

Beer in a café, kissing when parting at the station, staring at the fields behind the compartment window.

At home there was a fight; during his milk delivery my father had seen that my classmates weren't in the museum at all but were cycling home after school. He forbade me to see the man again; from then on I was no longer allowed to leave the house after school. My mother did not get involved. Her straight back expressed nothing. Was she thinking of her own decision about her life? She didn't want to protect or condemn me.

At school it became exciting. We made love in an unused classroom, during class we spoke in a poetic secret language, and we tucked letters in each other's bags. I told no one. The day after the final examination I stood on his doorstep in Amsterdam, carrying a suitcase filled with books and clothes.

Five o'clock. Harry rang the bell. He had a bag with sandwiches ready in the car. I took the book I was to read from, and we left. Usually I'm hungry at that time of day, but the prospect of Delft tightened my throat and numbed my stomach. Harry was making a mess, and I pushed a newspaper on his lap on which pieces of tomato and bits of white cheese were falling. Aalsmeer, Leimuiden, The Hague.

It was a disaster, of course. The plan had not been for me to hang on to him and be unwilling to be dragged out of his bed. Luckily I've always figured out very quickly when I was too much. I have forgotten the teacher, but I've retained the poems and Vermeer. In Zurich and later in Boston I studied spaces. I designed buildings in which you could imagine yourself outside while you were inside. During my vacations I went looking for paintings by Vermeer and, holding my breath, I looked at the inside of his private homes in which silent women stood waiting with royal calm.

From the car, Harry phoned his mother in the old people's home. The attendant had just brought her a tray with dinner, and Harry asked her to lift the lids and describe the food.

"Meatballs rolled in bacon," he said, "just leave it, Ma, you don't like it." I heard a creaky voice coming out of the telephone, but I couldn't understand the words.

"I'm off to Delft, Ma," said Harry, "I'll call you back later, before you go to sleep."

The polders lay in an eerie yellow afternoon light of the kind that shines from under leaden clouds. The sea of grass began to exert a pull on me; I would have liked to get out and then go through those meadows by myself, alone. The shining water in the ditches, the small differences in water levels on either side of the dykes, the thick clumps of grass on the banks—all that increased a desire within me to lie down.

"You look as if you're going to your death," said Harry as he turned off the freeway. I held my hands in a chilly knot in front of my chest, my knees trembled. He doesn't understand it at all, I thought. I should never have started on this, let myself be persuaded, be bullied. Via Oosteinde we drove to the Markt. Blood pounded in my head, and when Harry had finally parked the car I was unable to get out. He brushed the crumbs off his clothes and turned towards me.

"How can a woman of your calibre be upset by such a lousy little town! Just explain that!"

I have never studied Vermeer's oeuvre in an art historical or technical sense, but I have always felt a curiously strong fascination for it.

As if it had or should have anything to do with me. In the parked car I felt like the girl drinking wine in her beautiful red dress, who stares into her glass and keeps drinking because she doesn't know what to say, can't think, doesn't know what the rules are. I found it difficult to give Harry the role of the interested, still friendly man who wants to refill her glass. He is so approachable and so completely the opposite of tall that I burst out laughing.

We got out of the car and decided to walk around a bit. The tower of the Oude Kerk stood crooked above the canal. If it fell, it would fit exactly between the brick edges and the water would rise like a stinking wall.

"The fact that they don't care for you," I tried, "that you don't belong. That you don't understand how they think. They know the rules and you never figure them out, no matter how you try. Because you are, in fact, no good." Harry nodded and was silent; he clasped the cell phone in his hand. I continued; I would never be able to explain it adequately but I floundered on, blindly, confused.

"There was no way out. There was an invisible dome over the city and you were imprisoned under it. If I whispered something in a friend's ear on Westvest, they knew it on Oostsingel. Once a year all the eleven- and twelve-year-old children walked to the Markt to sing songs there for a whole hour. The conductor danced on a wooden podium, his black hair hung in strands in front of his face, and his hands drew in the air the lines that we had to sing. Liberation, I thought, but the sound from the hard children's throats rebounded, could not bore a hole in the dome. You could get out through the polders at the edge of the city. If you turned around at the end of the afternoon, you saw Delft lying there, beckoning sternly with its two fingers. Oh well, Harry, I really did my best but I've never understood it."

We ended up on Beestenmarkt, formerly an out-of-bounds area. Here sheep and calves had stood kicking against the wooden pens that had been placed between the poles. Death hung over it. In the cafés farmers shouted for drink. Children had no business being there.

The poles with their grooves were still standing, otherwise the square was unrecognizable. Swaying crowns of trees above terraces, cheerful people at the table under coloured parasols, music.

Harry checked out the places to eat and led me to a chair which stood with its back against the wall. The waiter was polite and good-natured. He filled Harry's orders quickly and pleasantly. I drank white wine which wasn't sour but cool and agreeably dry.

"Sometimes the school doctor would come," I said suddenly. "A weird man with a head full of dandruff who received us one after the other in the principal's office. You had to take off your shoes and socks and walk to and fro for him. He tapped on your back and looked to see whether you had breasts yet. Afterwards he washed his hands in the washbasin and you could leave. I was always afraid that I would be declared unfit, but I never knew for what."

"Just drink," said Harry. "Everything is completely different now."

He had coded his mother's number into the cell phone so that he needed to press only one button to get in touch with the old people's home.

"They'll come and get the tray right away, Ma. Just leave it. Turn the television on now, it's starting soon, you haven't missed anything yet." The telephone made creaking, rasping sounds.

"She's going to watch *The Bold and the Beautiful*," he said as he put the telephone in his inside pocket. "She does that every day. Sometimes I watch with her. A good soap."

He ate with relish: carpaccio, steak, apple pie. After-wards he had a stomach ache. I ordered tomato soup and left half of it. The sun disappeared behind the façades.

All too quickly we were standing on the Grote Markt, a stone expanse, bordered on the right by the façade of the Nieuwe Kerk, on the left by the City Hall that looked like a fairy-tale castle with its small square tower and its cheerful shutters. I told Harry that there, in front of the steps, they had carried out death sentences; blood lay between those stones. He placed his hand on my back and steered me diagonally across the Markt in the direction of the tribunal, the scaffold, the executioner.

I'm not writing you because of an unstable mental condition. For several years I've been completely stable and, despite my demanding activities, I'm not over-stressed.

However, I have been alone since that time. Perhaps that is for me the only way to keep my balance. The word *"over-stressed"* doesn't do justice to my condition before the present equilibrium set in. I flew around the world at breakneck speed, from a project in Jakarta to a lecture series in Los Angeles, working, writing, talking, waking. I had left my husband, had left home and marriage and was adrift. It had taken me ten years to figure out that I could not be permanently with someone. As soon as I was safe I seeped out, so to speak, through the closed shutters. A shadow of a woman remained behind, and he couldn't put up with that. Not that I saw it like that at the time. I blamed him. Everything that detracted from total devotion I interpreted as unfaithfulness and abandonment. When he went to wash himself after making love, I felt rejected. I held on to him so that I wouldn't have to flee, but I didn't know that at the time. Without wanting to, I became a copy of my mother who, estranged, stood straight-backed in her own kitchen, was unable to change the bond with my father into the language of everyday life and kept longing for an unreal period of her past in which she had been lifted beyond herself for a moment.

Harry rubbed my back with his big hand. He made me walk ahead and whispered in my ear.

"Don't say a thing. I know how it feels. Shall I tell you how I handle it? Harry's secret recipe, especially for you. You have to be polite. Friendly. Remember their names. Ask about their children, their jobs, their disgusting hobbies. You have lay it on thick until they can no longer move. Only then do you strike, in a restrained way. You leave them behind with their knees ensnared in compliments, with their heads confused by praise. You have to keep looking clever to be sure they despise you but still are afraid of you. And always keep smiling. Politeness is a golden dagger."

Meanwhile we had climbed up the steps and were busy with greetings. I smiled and shook various hands. Because I was thinking about what Harry had just whispered to me, I couldn't remember the names that I heard. The woman who was obviously responsible for the arrangements had been waiting for us at the top of the stairs and was continually blaring into my ears about committee members, architects, the mayor. I could place that last one, he was wearing the chain of office around his neck. He looked at me with friendly, melancholy eyes.

"Welcome home, Mrs Lievaert," he said. My eyes were stinging. The woman pulled at my sleeve and continued reciting titles and names. Finally she led me to a small room where the Crown Prince sat smoking a cigarette which he stubbed out quickly when we entered. With him, too, I exchanged a handshake, a meaningless word or two. Harry had remained standing in the hall. He winked at me and took my elbow when I came out of the small room.

I was still musing about his desperate friendliness offensive. It surprised me that he, the champion-arranger, the one who managed to get everything he had set his heart on, who didn't seem to be cowed by any confrontation, was scared enough to imagine how he would resist and could even put this into words in peace and quiet. The mother, the stomach ache. Poor Harry.

Giving a reading is nice. You don't have to think up anything new for it, the text is ready, nothing can really go wrong. The only thing you have to do is to believe in your own text. You wait. You stretch the silence. You speak, you find the right rhythm, the right tempo. When you've found that, you notice that the audience breathes with you. Never speak too fast. Never go on too long, always read a few minutes less than was agreed. Make sure there is good lighting, a lectern on which to place your hand, some water.

The invited guests sat on seats resembling church benches that had been placed in the hall in a herringbone pattern. The mayor welcomed everyone. The prince, in the first row, smiled and crossed his enormous legs. Across from the majestic entrance, the room was bordered by a wall of pillars. Behind them Harry walked back and forth on his crepe soles. Sitting for a long time made him restless. I sat at the end of the front bench, next to a pillar. I folded my hands over my book of poems and listened to the speeches as if they were music, without having to understand anything. From behind the pillars I heard a soft squeaking and from the corner of my eye I saw Harry walk to the back, the telephone at his ear. The poetry book slid to the floor. I bent forward, stretched out my arm and saw a large, well-formed man's hand lie next to mine on the book. Short nails, medium hairy. Blue and white striped cuff, dark grey wool sleeve. No watch, no ring. I turned my head sideways and looked into a face all eyebrows and lips, dark tanned like that of an outdoorsman, a gypsy, a hunter. I pulled back my hand. He put the book on my knees again and smiled as he touched my arm lightly. Without thinking I pressed my hand for a moment against his upper leg; through the fabric of his suit I felt the muscles, thinner, sturdier than I had surmised. Here you are. Thank you. I slumped back on the bench.

As soon as there was a break, Harry dashed towards me. He looked pale and was talking as he advanced.

"I have to leave. Ma has suddenly become ill, her heart, she's gone to hospital, I'm going there at once. Can you manage? Here's your money, take a taxi to Amsterdam, I'm sorry, I *have* to go, *now!*"

He crumpled some bank notes into my hand. Sweat stood on his forehead.

"Of course I'll manage," I said. "Getting out of here will be no problem." I saw my neighbour's face before me, how he would bend over the car door, in parting would smile through the window. Harry breathed fast and unevenly.

"Are you all right?' I asked. "Will you drive carefully?"

I took him to the door and walked outside with him, onto the steps. I wanted to take him to the car but he stopped me.

"Please, do go in, these people are waiting for you. Do your duty!"

I watched him as he crossed the Markt diagonally, so fast that he was almost running, clasping the telephone in one hand, the car keys pointing ahead in the other.

I stood on the threshold and listened to the swimming pool-like racket of hundreds of simultaneous conversations. In small circles people swarmed together, tapered glasses and sometimes a cigarette in their hands. In the circle around the Crown Prince I recognized the mayor and my attentive neighbour. They were deep in conversation and made exaggerated gestures. He looked up, my neighbour, saw me and waved.

The lady from the organization walked to the back, and a few moments later a gong sounded. Slowly the audience slid onto the benches. The talking rippled to a lower frequency and came to a stop when the chairman introduced me.

I read the series of ten poems about Delft, about

Vermeer. The light was good, the audience was quiet. I realized that I was there, that my feet stood on the tiles on which Vermeer had also stood, that I had taken up position in the heart of the city, standing straight, and that I was speaking words, my words.

All in all my reading lasted no more than fifteen minutes. The applause was thundering, as if the tension of the still poems had to be broken violently. I bowed my head in thanks, pressed my book against my chest and walked to my seat at the end of the first row. My neighbour put a large, white handkerchief in his pocket, bent towards me and placed his warm hand on mine. He nodded as if he wanted to say: yes, the way you just expressed it, that's how it is, yes exactly like that. He understands something, I thought. He gave me a serious smile which I fully accepted.

People often smile at me and mostly I don't know how to handle it. I fall silent and look away. I don't believe in compliments because I distrust the motives of the person giving the compliments. If it is necessary to continue the conversation, I switch to a different subject. More than anything most people prefer to talk about themselves and they do that easiest, and I feel comfortable with it; that way I can keep out of range.

This was different. This man made me believe that he really meant what he said. Or rather: what he did, for he actually said nothing. Contented, I sat through the rest of the evening, next to the pleasant, even warmth of my neighbour.

After the lectures in the city hall, a reception was held in a house on one of the canals.

The Crown Prince was led out. Enormous cars drove up to the front to carry away the guests. I stood next to my neighbour looking out over the illuminated market square, at the statue of Hugo de Groot in the middle circle, at the slender façade of the Nieuwe Kerk across the way. We drank champagne. The air was cool, the stone of the stairs exuded the heat of the day; it was a perfect summer evening without wind.

"We're going on to have a drink at someone's home, one of the sponsors, I think. We would appreciate it very much if you would come with us," said the organization lady. I joined the small group of people strolling around in front of the city hall stairs. Except for my neighbour I knew no one, but I didn't care. I was in Delft, I was at home and I felt an inexplicable calm.

The streets were quiet, the city seemed deserted. All the sour people had been put to bed and slept. My neighbour clasped my elbow and guided me behind the group that was walking away, around the city hall, past the covered fish market that spread sea air from behind the green shutters, across a bridge, on the way to a canal. I had drunk at least three glasses of champagne and let myself be led over the small cobblestones without paying attention to the route. I had cast aside all distrust and vigilance. We looked inside under the archway of the Prinsenhof. Heavy tree tops

hung dark over the deathly quiet square. Sit on a bench
there, I thought, motionless, nothing but silence.

He put his arm around my shoulders and led me
along the canal. In the distance a door stood open; a path
of yellow light lay on the pavement, and as we came closer
we heard soft music.

Yes, I went in, I entered that canal house which was much
larger than you would expect from the outside. Probably
up a staircase, into a drawing room where people were
already drinking. I remember that I went around a corner
and ended up on a covered terrace where a perfect chair
was standing. There he had me sit down, with a glass. He
disappeared behind me into the room, and I was alone. I
took off my shoes, I stretched my arms and looked at the
dark gardens far below. Way over on the right I thought I
could distinguish the cloister garden of the Prinsenhof, but
I don't know that for sure, it's almost impossible. Suddenly
I needed a cigarette to underline the fact that I had won a
battle. Smoke signals, a peace pipe, fear that smoulders into
ashes. From a silver cup I took one; I lit it with a flame of
a candle that stood flickering on the small table next to me.
I leaned back and inhaled the spicy smoke. I was not dizzy,
not drunk, not alienated. Still, I was a stranger in a house
that I didn't know, with a man whom I had never seen
before, drinking and smoking at an hour when I was usually
in bed.

I was content, Mr Kallander, I had unlimited confidence in the course of events. I listened to what could be heard: silence from the garden down below, low rumbling men's voices from the room behind me, an outburst of laughter, footsteps on an old parquet floor. All embedded in music that I recognized but couldn't place. Mozart, an opera, very soft, so as not to disturb the conversations.

I might have dozed off for a moment; I know that I had closed my eyes to experience the sounds better. Suddenly he sat next to me and gave me a fresh glass. He had rolled up his shirtsleeves; I saw the hairs on his lower arms and noticed that the conversations had ceased. Only Mozart could be heard. Now I knew what it was: Leporello was singing the catalogue aria. I was silent, I waited for the beautiful ending when he sings to Elvira cynically but with great compassion that she should know, that she herself has experienced how he does it, how he seduces a woman and offers his heart. And not only to her, but also to one thousand and three others: surely you know, surely you knew. I smiled. I knew too, but it didn't matter. I went along with pleasure and curiosity.

"They're gone," he said. "We're alone."

He left again. I heard water splash and glasses rattle. My body felt loose and lithe, the linen jacket was cool on my skin. He had stroked my hair when he came in. The touch stayed with me for a long time, as if senses, nerves and brains were reluctant to give up the impression.

A caressed woman listened to Mozart on a terrace in Delft.

You should know, Kallander, that I don't make it a habit to sleep with men whom I have known for only one evening. Whose name I wasn't even able to remember. Still, I did it that night. Drink, you'll say, too much champagne and too little food. Maybe even a psychedelic cigarette without realizing it. Poets are naïve unrealistic people, otherwise they wouldn't be able to write poetry.

    Nonsense, my reality testing was completely fine; I wasn't at all under the influence and I knew exactly what I was doing. I appreciated that man, I enjoyed his attention, I had to laugh at his comments, I felt at home with his body. Not for a moment did I then, on the terrace, or afterwards, in the bedroom, think about the fact that I didn't know his name. You, I thought. That was enough. Not until later, when it was all over, did I notice that I had no name for him. The organizer had named so many names that my head was reeling from the most dazzling, exotic, dramatic, hilarious names (Jean de Bassiès, Victor Fourcat, Pierre de Balledreyt?); they flashed through my head without attaching themselves to anything. I hadn't listened, I was still afraid and wanted it to be over, I was worried about Harry and longed for a quiet room in which to be alone for a moment. Later, yes, later I was sorry about my inattention, but not yet that night.

The bedroom, I said. How we had landed there? No idea. The lights in the drawing room were turned off, thin white curtains blew in from the terrace like cobwebs, Leporello had finished singing. A small trip is etched in my memory, deeper into the house: a half staircase, going through an extension situated to one side? The room in which we ended up was dark and tall, as large as a second drawing room. Behind the inside doors I assumed there were windows to the canal; the room where the bed stood had a large window on the side of the garden.

What should I tell you, Mr Kallander? Nothing, surely? I think only of you, with your emaciated body in white cotton underwear underneath an age-old tweed suit; I carry on an imaginary conversation with you, of which a very small censored part will end up in my letter to you. It's none of your business. The secret of the bed is not the secret that I want to share with you. Let it suffice that it was as it should be. He had a strong but modest body on which I saw white shorts outlined in the subdued light. Fortunately not an exhibitionist who pulls off his pants at the slightest occasion. Everything went smoothly. He stroked my foot, he took my foot in his warm hand when he was in me.

Lying under the thin sheet, we talked. Alas, I can't remember much of it. I think that he said he worked in London and was sometimes here over the weekend. I classified him

among the sponsors and thought of the nearby Zestien-
hoven airport. A businessman or banker who wanted to
experience the seventeenth century in his spare time. I
stroked the hairs on his arms, on the back of his hands,
and was almost asleep when he started talking in another
tone. Compelling, suddenly serious, obsessed.

He had chosen me, he said. For years he had followed
me, read all my work, seen every interview. Oh no, I
thought, not that, I don't want that during this perfect
night. But it was something else. Something that burdened
him, something that delighted him, something that he had
never told nor shown to anyone. He had chosen me to
share the secret. I didn't have to do anything about it, I
was free. The thing for him was that he wouldn't be the
only one who knew it.

"Why me?" I asked. I leaned on my arm and looked
intently at his face.

"Vermeer," he answered. "When you read tonight, you
looked exactly like the woman reading a letter. So concentrated, so calm. Then I knew for sure: I'll show it to you."

The way you take a child seriously, a child who comes
running from school, panting and almost stuttering with
agitation, wanting to show you something that is of vital
importance for him—you acknowledge his feeling, you go
along with his view of the matter as serious, you get up
immediately and let yourself be pulled along by his warm,

impatient hand. Perhaps you feel a slight curiosity; you also feel a slight annoyance because this urgency pulls you from your contemplation, from your reading. You'd almost want to shrug your shoulders, want to say something to put it into perspective, but you restrain yourself for the sake of the child's enthusiasm. You don't want to hurt him, but you're already looking forward to the moment when you can sit down again, light a cigarette, pick up your book. His enthusiasm matters to you, but the object of his passion will not touch your world. That's what you think. You start off like this, half-amused, half-sighing, behind your agitated, purposeful guide.

We put on threadbare bathrobes. He grabbed a bunch of keys from a drawer and motioned with his head. In the hall he took my hand. Barefoot we went up stairs, down stairs, through rooms, past a poorly lit landing, a gallery, a spiral staircase. To an attic, definitely to a room situated higher. There was a door with a heavy lock into which he stuck the key. Before pulling the oak panel towards him, he embraced me. He stroked my face, kissed my eyelids, pressed me so vehemently against him that I almost couldn't breathe. Then he opened the door.

First I saw nothing. An empty attic with wooden beams, lit by skimpy light bulbs near the entrance. There was a dark rear wall, with stains, folds of a cloth.

"Stay there, eyes closed!"

He let go of me and I heard the soles of his feet slap on the wood, curtain rings slide over a rod, a switch click. I heard him inhale rapidly. Then I looked.

I estimate that the painting I saw there is a little over three feet high and two and a half feet wide. There is no frame. The picture is dominated by the figure of a man who, bent forward slightly, stands in front of a table and washes his hands in a bowl. Behind his head a stained glass window opened to the inside is visible. A diagonal runs from about 8 inches in from the upper left corner down to the bottom right of the canvas. The space to the left of this diagonal is occupied by the man's body. The canvas is cut off at the level of his thighs. He is wearing a green coat. His hat lies on a table next to the water jug.

Kallander, undoubtedly you know the phenomenon where you disappear while looking at a painting that grabs you by the throat. I think that I took a dozen steps forward, stopping four or five feet from the canvas. I think that my breathing calmed down and became smooth, regular and normal. I think so, but I don't know. There is no memory of stance, feeling in muscles, eye movements. There is only the awareness of the green coat, a green with a hint of blue; the amazement at the drops of water that fall from the folded hands into the bowl; the awareness of Vermeer. I was in the painting, I was one with it, and I don't know how long that lasted.

The right side of the picture shows a room in perspective, seen through an open door. The colours change: from the cool, blue-green of the coat via the black and white tiles on the floor and the brownish doorpost, to an ebony bench along the wall of the room in the back. On the bench sits a woman, also depicted in profile, slumped back with legs apart, her head leaning against the wall. She is wearing a yellow jacket, the yellow jacket with the fur collar. Her blond hair has been pulled away tightly from her face into a small bun on the top of her head. Her arms rest across her thighs, hands dangling onto her lap. The eyelids, of the whitest ivory, are shut.

After hours, days, eternities, probably not even fifteen minutes, I became aware that he was standing behind me. I heard him breathe heavily through his nose, I felt his warmth when he came closer, and I leaned against his body. He threw his arms around me and put his chin on my head. This way we looked, this time together, at the man with a head of curly hair that reached his shoulders. He had pulled the wide cuffs of his coat up slightly so that the thin wrists and hands were free. He looked with deep concentration at the water that dripped from his fingers. Next to the broad-brimmed hat a white towel lay on the front part of the table. Ample, folded, a wall of snow that enclosed the painting.

"This doesn't exist," I said. "It is a Vermeer, but this one doesn't exist."

He sighed, blowing my hair upwards. He freed his

arm from around me and pointed to the transom above the door in the painting. I squinted my eyes and the vague letters became clear: IVMeer.

I wanted him to hold me again, I wanted to be completely surrounded and feel solidity on all sides. I didn't believe what I saw, but I did see it.

"These are two houses; I bought two houses next to each other. When I broke through behind the façades, I found it, in a hollow wall. Folded in a piece of leather, a cowhide, standing up straight between the two sides of the wall. When the workers had left, I took a closer look. It was the strangest evening of my life."

I wanted to say something but couldn't produce a word. I was filled with all sorts of thoughts but couldn't concentrate on any. Why had he not revealed his find? Was it a criminal offence to keep such a painting to yourself? Was he, as owner of the houses, also owner of the painting? What did he want with it? Why did he show it to me? What if a fire started in the attic? What comes next after you have seen it?

Like wisps of smoke the questions blew from my head. I looked, I devoured the painting with my eyes until I was satiated. Then we turned around, closed the door, and went back to bed.

Of course I thought that I had dreamed everything when I woke up and saw the painting against my closed eyelids.

I continued to lie very still and looked. Then I opened my eyes.

I lay in bed alone, in an airy room with opened curtains. He was gone. On the floor lay two entangled bathrobes.

I sat bolt upright and threw off the sheets. A pale note fluttered up: "Sorry, I have to leave early. Don't want to wake you. Thank you, thank you, thank you!"

Alone in a strange house. I put on my clothes, grabbed my bag which stood by the door, and found my way out. In a hall I found a bathroom. I slammed a front door shut behind me and hurried to the station. There were no taxis. I bought a train ticket and sat down to wait on the platform. It was ten o'clock.

From behind the protective compartment window I looked at the city rolling away: Wesseling dance school, the mill, the yeast factory. It wasn't until the train rolled into the polders that I sat back. I had no opinion. I had expected to be able to look back to an exciting, secret night without consequences, but the only thing I could think of was the painting. First go home, I thought, a bath, coffee, clean clothes, start the day. Rinse off the night. Wash my hands.

From the outset, the painting looked like a real Vermeer to me and made an absolutely authentic impression. I therefore ask you the question: what have I seen?
    Sincerely,
    Helena Lievaert

And what should I do now? Should I do anything, is this letter already too much? What can such a man write back about it? What good is it to him? Information, he has to gather information, he is a scholar. It doesn't have to be of any use to him, it should be of use to me. Suggestions, an explanation, help.

I closed the envelope and put a stamp on it. Storm in The Hague tomorrow.

Before leaving for Switzerland to give my yearly series of seminars, I called Harry. His voice sounded weak and all questions in the conversation came from my side. How was his mother doing? He sighed, there was little improvement. She was still in the hospital, her heartbeat was visible and audible on a monitor and he, Harry, had to endure that while he sat with her. Every day, and at night too, he said. That incessant ticking on the screen got on his nerves. It caused him to make terrible scenes with the staff about the food they planned to serve his mother. Usually he brought something along for her; he knew what she liked, those caregiving types didn't. Mother had no appetite. She was afraid, everything was scary; that doesn't make food attractive.

It wasn't until we had discussed at length the misery that made him powerless that he asked me how it had been in Delft.

"Fine," I said. "It really went fine, it was even rather

nice. No problems, I got home safely. I'll tell you another time, when your mother is better."

I told him I'd be gone for the next two weeks and promised to call him when I was back. I would take care of the mail myself, or leave it for him.

"Have a good trip," said Harry, "and take good care of yourself. Call me if you need anything; I always have the telephone with me."

I still wanted to tell him how sorry I felt for him and that I didn't expect him to do any work for me for the time being—but he had already hung up. I missed him. I would have liked to tell him my story, but I didn't know if I was allowed to talk about it. Perhaps it was just as well this way, and I had to carry the secret with me on my trip.

Coming home after a long trip is a dubious pleasure. I relish the prospect of being alone once again. In every hotel, no matter how good, cleaning staff and chambermaids come and rattle your door at all hours of the day. Every trip means: contact. With students, with organizers, with people who are associated with me, or at least with my work. That oppresses me. I feel that so much attention is excessive. Of course I do my best and try to say something interesting in my classes; of course I write my poems and essays as well and as honestly as possible; still, I find it strange that people can be so uncritically enthusiastic. Then I think it's because they have paid for my visit. It's expensive, so it should be worth something. Because I have a name. They lap up everything from me because the name Lievaert is on it, just as I devour everything that has Nabokov on it, just as a cow in any meadow bends towards the grass because it is green. These thoughts start after about a week and don't leave me until I step back into my own house. In my chair, with a stack of old newspapers on my lap, with the freedom to ignore the telephone and to plan my own day, I can realize once again that I write because I write and that everyone is free to make of it what he or she thinks. It doesn't have to bother me.

The disadvantage of coming home, especially when Harry isn't there, is the mail. Carefully I slide the knife into the first envelopes. Soon I pull out the letters, unrestrained. I make a stack that requires further action and a stack of trash.

This is how, that Sunday afternoon just back from Switzerland, I sat rustling and juggling with papers until I held in my hand a heavy letter with a discreet imprinted stamp of the sender: the Cabinet of the Golden Age.

Dear Mrs Lievaert,

In answer to your surprising letter I can inform you that there did indeed exist a painting by Vermeer as described by you. It is mentioned in the catalogue of the so-called Dissius auction which was held in Amsterdam in 1696. The description is as follows: "Where a lord washes his hands in a see-through room, with figures artful and rare."

Since that time, nothing more has been heard of this painting, which was priced as one of the most expensive at that auction. No other descriptions and no copies of it are known. The painting is considered lost, and this makes it exceptionally unlikely that you have seen it. However, your description has made me curious, and I am prepared to view the canvas in question and to appraise it if the owner so desires.

Assuming that you will inform me about this, I remain sincerely,

E. Kallander

I let the letter drop in my lap. A "see-though" room, "artful and rare"—exactly what I had seen. "A lord who washes his hands"—you couldn't describe it more succinctly or more simply. The realization that this painting, which had vanished without a trace for three centuries, was hanging in an attic in a canal house in Delft where I could just walk, made me gasp. I had to do something. I had to find out his name, call, write, meet him.

In Harry's well-organized correspondence files I found the telephone number of the conference organization. Don't hesitate, do it right away. I got a young man on the phone and asked for the lady who had been in charge of the final event.

"You mean Mrs Muysch?"

I didn't know, it could be, I had no idea, but affirmed

decisively. In the background I heard melodious, questioning voices and a door slamming shut.

"Ella Muysch!"

"Yes, Helena Lievaert."

"How nice of you to call. You are on my list. I wanted to thank you again for your delightful contribution to the conference. Everyone enjoyed it *so much*, you should see how many enthusiastic comments we have received!"

I tried to interrupt by coughing and clearing my throat. I'm so bad at telephoning. But something finally started to register with Mrs Muysch.

"Are you calling for a special reason? I hope that nothing went wrong with the administration? Of course you can still declare any travel expenses, that's a matter of sending the taxi receipt, I'll take care of it. The honorarium, yes, it's possible that it hasn't been credited to your account yet because we've been very busy here. We have to wrap up everything and draw up the balance sheet, and that's more work than we thought. We've been inundated by paperwork for weeks!"

"No," I said, "that's not what it's about. I'm sure that all that will be straightened out. I was wondering, after the evening programme there was a sort of reception, you remember, on one of the canals, a house, at someone's house."

"Yes, that was on Oude Delft. I escorted the Crown Prince out and then walked along with the mayor. So nice when it's all behind you, certainly when it was such a success, such a load off your shoulders. The Prince was very enthusiastic!" Mrs Muysch laughed, clucking.

"But at whose house, at whose house was it? I would like to know the name of the person at whose house the reception took place. You did introduce me to everyone, but that name has escaped me. I would like to get in touch with the man, but I don't remember his name."

That was not appreciated. Mrs Muysch was the one who got in touch or not, not I. Moreover, I seemed to have hit a weak spot. Her voice lowered a notch and lost its excited expression.

"Well, I don't know if I can help you with that," she said sternly. "That reception was an improvised event as far as I know. It didn't fall under our management at any rate. I assumed that the host represented one of our sponsors. If you wish, I could give you the address of our board member who is responsible for the sponsors."

"Please." I scribbled the address of the cover of the telephone book.

"I hope that you are successful in your inquiries," Mrs Muysch said formally. "Good day."

"I beg your pardon, please excuse me!" Spluttering, the words flew out of my mouth. "Do you perhaps have a telephone number for that board member?"

Pow pow pow pow pow pow. Like bullets the numbers rang into my ear. Sweating, I put down the receiver.

In the evening, after a bottle of red wine, I had gathered
enough courage to pick up the telephone once again. The
recruiter of sponsors turned out to be a friendly man who
couldn't help me either. He was under the impression that
the party had been given at the house of one of the partici-
pating architects. Neither the board members nor the sponsors had anything to do with it. He had been there himself
for a short while and affirmed that the house was situated
on Oude Delft. He could no longer remember the host
very well.

"By that time I had drunk quite a bit, the recollection
of that evening has become rather hazy."

"He sat next to me, that man of the house," I said,
"in the first row, way over on the side. A tall man, he was
there the whole evening and spoke to everyone, you must
know him."

But he had said that this memory for faces was not
very good. Floor plans, numbers, those were no problem,
but people?

"Would the mayor know?" I tried. "He stood talking
with him for a long time." The sponsor recruiter started to
laugh.

"Oh, Mrs Lievaert, that mayor of ours! He is an exceptionally friendly person, really a first-class mayor, but he
doesn't know whether he's coming or going. He can remember nothing, absolutely nothing. He doesn't even know his
secretary's name. You don't notice it much because he's so
incredibly charming. He speaks to strangers as if they were

good friends. And when there are important visitors, there's always someone whispering into his ear. No, I wouldn't count on the mayor in this instance. It's too bad that I can't help you, I would have done so with pleasure. I do hope you're not terribly disappointed?"

I blushed. He thinks I'm looking for a date, that I'm after that guy. He's making fun of me. During the next board meeting he will gossip about me with Mrs Muysch. How awful.

I thanked him for his helpfulness and hung up. That night I dreamed of the painting, which I could approach without any difficulty. I saw how the light from the open window fell on the cheeks of the man washing his hands. I stood so close that I could see his nostrils, his eyelashes, the wrinkled skin of his mouth.

111

Kallander's letter was burning on my desk. He was counting on me to take some action. I had to do something. The quest was at a standstill and I had to think of a new approach. I had to, I had to. But how? I didn't know at all how to go about it. If only Harry were here.

My thoughts kept going round and round fruitlessly, from morning till night. I didn't get much work done. I read a bit, organized my papers, sat staring absent-mindedly. I called Harry who also seemed absent-minded, weary. He sounded tired and I left him alone.

I tried to imagine Delft at night and walked time after

time from the City Hall to the canal. The dark shutters of the fish market. The path of light from the front door. The unlit window of the bookstore. Yes!

The next day I was back at the station. It was Delft weather; it drizzled and the clammy air struck my face. Without looking right or left, I walked to the bookstore and at the counter asked to speak to the owner. Before the cashier could even call her, she appeared from behind a giant stack of cardboard boxes. She recognized me immediately.

"How nice of you to stop by! Really sold a lot the other day. And you're still selling full blast. Do you want some coffee?"

She was slightly younger than myself. An enterprising, independent woman who did her best to smuggle books into the households of Delft and to bring about a broadening of horizons. She didn't take heed of anything and went her own way, whether Delft liked it or not. Be informal, I thought, those are the rules here, go ahead, you're here, you can leave, there's no real danger.

"I'll be back in an hour," she said to the girl behind the cash register. In the store some students were reading, leaning against the book cases. They didn't look up.

"Yes, I also run a library," she said, smiling. "I don't mind, it fills the store and later, when they have money, they'll come and buy things. Don't you think?"

We sat down in a café with enormous windows, across

from a bridge; the traffic seemed to be roaring straight towards us.

"View of Delft," she said. "Why did you actually come?"

I didn't have the nerve. I waited until the coffee was served, until the waiter walked away, until we were stirring our coffee.

"I'm looking for a man," I said.

She burst out laughing.

"Well, then you're really at the right address! I have dozens on special—just come and sit behind the cash register one afternoon. But you don't really mean it, you can't be in need of a man? Aren't things fine without one?"

"Yes, no, I don't mean it like that." I stumbled and stuttered. I had to think more carefully. What do I want to know? That's what I should ask. Straightforward.

"There was a man sitting next to me. Later he gave a party. What is his name?"

The bookseller narrowed her eyes.

"I see him in front of me. Tall. A little bit the type: I can't help being here, but really nice. Not awful. You seemed to be having a great time with him. Did you go to that party?"

"Yes," I answered to everything. "But I paid so little attention that I forgot where it was and what his name was. I was hoping that you would know. I want to ask him something."

"I don't know him. Never saw him before either. He's

never been in the store. I saw you walk along the canal when I was returning the books. She had invited me, that bag from the organization, but I was firm, I had to get up early the next day, I simply went to bed. Was it nice?"

I reported: beautiful house, nice conversation, soft evening, much alcohol, lovely night. I also told her about my attempts to discover the man's identity. She confirmed the doubts about the mayor's memory and smirked at my report of the telephone conversation with Stella Muysch.

"People don't exist unless she's discovered them," she said. "I wouldn't expect anything from that office of hers. I'll put out feelers in the coming days. I'll call you."

On the way to the station I walked past the whole west side of the canal, stopping in front of every façade. It meant nothing to me, I didn't recognize any door.

At home there was another ivory-white letter from Kallander in my mailbox. For the progress of science it was of the utmost importance to track down the provenance of the painting. What was the status of my attempts to approach the presumptive owner? He, Kallander, was hoping to hear from me as soon as possible, otherwise he would call me. I placed the letter at the bottom of a stack of mail requiring an answer. I was at an utter loss. Disconnect the telephone? Nail the mailbox shut? Move? But I wanted to see the painting again too. Wasn't it my own quest? Why couldn't I let myself be helped like any normal person?

Why did I always assume that everyone thought I was difficult, deceitful, dissipated?

"Muysch isn't happy with you," the bookseller said on the telephone. "She thinks that you're making fun of her organizational talents and that you are poaching on her territory. In my opinion, she's carrying on like that because she can't stand not knowing the answer to your question. Just imagine, Stella Muysch not knowing someone, an important someone, for whom another celebrity is looking! She can't stand that. She snapped at me too. 'You with your contacts,' she said. As if I'm running a brothel!"

I asked her if she had found out any more.

"My dear girl, he has vanished, that lover of yours. No one knows him, no one knows who or where he is or what he was doing there. I think you should forget about him. It's hopeless."

She also thinks that I'm looking for a guy and that I can't take a rejection, I thought. For a moment I considered telling her all about the Vermeer. She would turn the whole of Delft upside down, inform the papers, bring in the police. I couldn't remember if I had promised secrecy, but I felt a distinct hesitation when I imagined taking her into my confidence. In that case, just play the pathetic middle-aged woman looking for companionship and erotic diversion. I thanked her. Lately I wasn't doing much besides thanking and inquiring, without any result. Polite until my jaws ached, listening without interest, in large fuzzy circles turning around the only thing that had made an impression on me: the painting.

When Kallander called me, I quickly made an appointment with him. I put on a dark grey suit and beforehand drummed into myself my only wish: finding the painting again. I wouldn't let myself be intimidated, I didn't want to be suspicious, I could no longer let myself be pushed into the role of sad and lonely single woman. Professional and independent, that was the motto.

His voice sounded somewhat hesitant, weak, and slightly hoarse, but not unpleasant. He would pick me up in an official car at the station in The Hague; from there we would drive to Delft together. I imagined how he would sit in the back seat with a plastic sandwich box on his lap, a napkin on his knees. I missed Harry. I was facing this all alone.

The agreed station exit was easy to find. The doors separated automatically and I stood outside. It was windy, and clouds kept moving across the sun so you couldn't tell whether it was warm or cold. Stupid that I hadn't taken along a raincoat or at least an umbrella. But I did have sunglasses, to hide behind if necessary.

Out of a dark blue BMW a short man rushed at me, waving his arms. He pumped my hand as he introduced himself: "Kallander. Good that you're here. Now we can start!" Strands of grey-blond hair lay across his head and on his nose were rimless glasses. He wasn't wearing a stinking old tweed jacket but a smart striped suit with a gold watch chain. Courteously, he held the door open for me, then walked briskly around the car and hopped energetically into his seat. Meanwhile I was already embarrassed at having said "Good afternoon, sir" to the chauffeur.

Kallander proceeded at once.

"You know Delft?" I nodded.

"How well?"

"I grew up here," I said through clamped jaws.

"Oh really, then you must know it inside out, that's nice. Did your father work at the Technical University?"

I shook my head. How could I shut that man up? Silence was clearly not the solution because the less I responded to his questions, the more Kallander talked. What did my parents do, what school had I attended, what street had I grown up in, how long had I been away from Delft, and why, and to where, and how often did I come back.

"That evening," I said, "when I saw the painting. That was the first time."

Did I visit my parents often, were they still alive, did they still live there, why had I given that reading, at whose invitation, where had I parked and at what time had I travelled back that evening? Alone or with others?

The problem was that all the questions were asked in an extremely polite and friendly manner. I considered myself increasingly rude because I didn't answer them adequately, as if it were proper to explain to a total stranger where you paid taxes, and how much, and with whom you had slept after a reading. I tried to push him back onto his own territory by asking with intense interest about his work in the Cabinet of the Golden Age. That gave me respite for a minute or so, but before I knew it he was on the subject of unsolicited letters and held forth about the stupid people who sent him trivial, paranoid, or totally invented stories about paintings, whether in their possession or not. I didn't know which way to look and put on my glasses.

The chauffeur parked on Phoenixstraat and we got out. There was a stiff wind which ruffled Kallander's strands of hair.

"Oude Delft, you're sure of that. Then I propose that we look at all the houses systematically. If your memory is correct, then this will surely lead to success."

I sweated like a pig despite the cooling breeze. Kallander set out at a brisk pace. I tried to tell him that I had already looked at all the houses, that I recognized nothing, that I didn't feel like it—but in vain. The plan had been made and had to be carried out. He stopped me in front of each façade and forced me to take in carefully the configuration of front door and windows and to compare it to the image in my memory.

"I don't have that clear an image," I said.

"Nonsense. According to what you say, you have been here, therefore there is an impression. It seems to me to be a question of willpower to get it back. The brain registers everything! A system! Concentration!"

After the third façade I started trembling with fear when I had to give him another no for an answer. Kallander's steps became measured and angry. Irritated, he pressed his thin lips together. Halfway along the canal, across from a tall, wide house, I wasn't sure. The front door seemed too low, I did remember steps, or was that only at the City Hall? The house had an attic, that was certain. Kallander was already pulling the bell. I stayed behind in the street and looked up, at the façade. On one of the upper floors a notice from a real estate agent hung in the window: For Sale.

No one answered; Kallander pulled me along and we continued with our fruitless project. On the way to the car I described the painting to him once more. He listened and kept quiet, for the first time that afternoon. It gave me the strength to shake his hand and to say that I had another appointment. He raised his eyebrows and opened his mouth to ask with whom, where, at what time—but I had already run off.

119

When the blue BMW had left with Kallander in the back seat, leafing angrily through the newspaper, I walked slowly to the station. I thought about how I had walked there twenty-five years earlier, next to my teacher, my lover, listening to his voice and hankering after his approval. How I had tried to distill guidelines for my behaviour from his words, how I had wished to be the way he wanted me to be. How all that had failed totally and how it felt. The wind lifted rubbish and leaves, people pressed their bags against themselves, women held their hands against their knees to hold their skirts in place. Everyone looked bitter and aggrieved. Everywhere noise, everywhere agitation.

"Just as before!" Harry shouted. "Fit as a fiddle! Nothing wrong! A hospital like that is an institution for torture, it brings on a heart attack, but now that she's home again —tip-top! She's eating again, she's watching her soaps again and she chats on the telephone. As before!"

He sat at my big table with the appointment book and the mail. I thought he looked bad: pale, and much heavier than a month ago. His mother's illness had really upset him; he would have to recover too. He gave me a detailed report about hospital life: the nurses who could not be bribed and who had wanted to impose their diet on his mother, the doctors who had frightened and mis-informed her.

"You're treated like garbage, like cattle, like a dog! Whisper to each other over her head, use words that no human being can understand. And their manners, carry on a conversation, say good-bye when they leave? Forget it. As soon as they've touched you, they go and disinfect their hands as if you have scabies. And don't imagine they feel like consulting with the family; they looked right through me, even though I sat there every day. When she was back in her own house, she recovered right away. And I did too. I feel good again." He banged his fist on the stack of mail. I imagined how he had sat helplessly at his mother's high bed and how his watertight friendliness offensive had run aground against the arrogant doctors. I was just as relieved as he was.

Harry put on his reading glasses and started opening the mail. I went to make coffee for us and heard him mumble while I rummaged in the kitchen.

"What do we have here?" he asked when I came in again. "Listen to this: 'I advise you urgently to ask for information at the land registry office about all home owners in the pertinent part of the canal area. I expect you to report to me within a week with the information in question.' What is that fellow thinking! To be ordering you around like that! What is this about?"

I recognized the Golden Age paper in his hand. There it was. I couldn't back out. I couldn't lie to Harry, I could never conceal anything from him.

I sat down and told him about the evening of the reading, the success of the performance, the champagne, my neighbour, the party, the love-making, the Vermeer. Harry listened to me as if I were telling him about a museum visit. He didn't think anything was strange, asked if I had liked it and said that my neighbour had looked like a nice guy.

121

"My mind was at ease when I left. He'll put her in a taxi, I thought."

I described my contacts with Kallander and my inability to satisfy his expectations.

"I can't break into all the houses on that canal. Or can I? The problem is that I want to find that painting, just as much as he does. And the longer this lasts, the more he thinks that I've just imagined something."

Harry was silent and peered through his glasses at Kallander's signature at the bottom of the letter. A deep, angry line with a dark blot at the end. I blew my nose and took a sip of coffee.

"Well?" he said finally. I said nothing in response. "Was it beautiful?"

"Perhaps the most beautiful thing I've ever seen. I still see it before me. Everything. I remember everything."

"Well, then you've got that," Harry said matter-of-factly. "Look, you're acting as if that museum fanatic has the final word, you let yourself be used by that bungler and you bend over backwards so that he'll like you—but why, actually? What do you care?"

Just as I had left Delft in the past, so in the same way I could step out of the evil web of expectations that Kallander had woven around me. I didn't like it, it was of no use to me, and I wouldn't be drawn and quartered if I ignored it. That's how simple it was.

Dear Mr Kallander,

 Unfortunately I am not in a position to follow up your suggestions. If you would like to continue investigations yourself, then I wish you success in that endeavour.

 Sincerely,

 Helena Lievaert

A simple note that I threw in the mailbox at once. Dancing, I ran back upstairs, gave Harry a kiss and reserved a table at his favourite restaurant. We drank to his mother's health.

 Ever since, I've been able to see the painting. It's mine; I can visit it whenever I want.

 I think of the women he painted, that dead citizen of Delft. The silent woman who looks out of the window, the one who fingers a pearl necklace, who hesitatingly strikes a seventh on the harpsichord. I know the man for whom she is waiting. I can draw his face; I would recognize the colour of his jacket anywhere.

 I have seen how she remains behind, how she leans idly against the wall. I see how he washes his hands in order to leave.

123

The injury

The sports park is on Vuurlinie. I get out of the car
on a windy Saturday afternoon. The soccer field is surrounded by a dyke and a low canteen. On the field our
boys are hopping about, still half under the influence from
last night but dressed in their fresh white shirts.

The team is not complete: one or two people took
the wrong bus or didn't hear their alarms.

Coach Arend is shouting good-humouredly. The
goalkeeper is afraid; one of the defenders hallucinates; the
striker lives in a dream world. Our son plays midfield. He
is good.

The opponents are better and on average fifteen years
older. Enormous, square men storm roaring at the slight

teenagers and time after time take away the ball with a shout. When Frits, who wears glasses, protests, a red-faced cattle driver threatens to attack him; the team clusters around the scuffle, then Arend calls out: "Easy, men!" Scared, Frits takes a step back.

I climb onto the grandstand where my husband and my daughter, the team mascot, are watching the game. I look into the distance and see a wide waterway behind the dyke, a sea of greenhouses around the sports complex and billboards on top of the canteen (Feed For Your Poultry; Theo Youngman, Barber).

The young team has not yet won a game but still has its camaraderie and enthusiasm. Our Willem and his friend Dirk run without complaining across the whole field to bring the ball to the desperate forwards; invariably something goes wrong in the forward line, and the opponents thunder like a herd of buffaloes towards the goal and the petrified goalkeeper.

"Make a play, that's the way," shouts Arend. "Cover your man, Joost, no, not that one, that's the ref."

Next to the playing field there is a fenced meadow with three horses in it. They gallop and kick up clumps of earth with their hooves. I hear shouting and quickly look back at the game. The boys have scored an unexpected goal. Foaming at the mouth, the crazed forward has run to the goal; between the legs of the goalkeeper, he stuffed the ball into the goal as the fullbacks watched in a daze. The referee didn't whistle, there was a confused silence and then a shrill cheering. Four-one.

The sky is leaden. Willem has taken control of the ball. The big man who threatened Frits comes stomping fast at him and extends his leg to touch the ball; Willem slides to the ground in an attempt to squeeze the ball through the columns of flesh. Then both players are lying on the grass.

Helped by his friends, Willem tries to stand up. Carefully he lets himself sink back down, leaning on his arms. We run to him and together carry him to the tiled floor in front of the locker room.

"I can't stand."

"Ice! Go and get ice!"

"Get the car," I say to Erik.

I storm into the forbidden territory of the lockers, empty the plastic rubbish bin on the floor and fill it with cold water; slowly I water my son's leg. Behind us one goal after the other is scored against the reduced team. Panting, Arend walks past: "I'll call you later!"

Willem looks pale when we lift him into the car. It starts to pour.

The cubicles in the emergency department are separated by curtains. Next to us we hear a man moaning continuously in a foreign language. Willem lies on a stretcher from which he has to be lifted again, with difficulty, for an X-ray.

Truth in the light box: a fracture of the tibia. The narrow fibula is intact. We wait.

"You've broken your leg," says the doctor. "The position is fairly good, we're putting it in a plaster cast and then you can go home."

A stocking is put on the leg up to the groin; it is rolled from a steel ring while two nurses lift the calf. Then the doctor starts working like a sculptor with the moistened plaster.

"Now it's safe," says Willem, but he blanches when the castmaster appears with the saw.

"It has to have a crack for when your leg swells." The saw screeches. Two grooves. With a screwdriver the castmaster prises pieces of plaster out of the crack.

Now Willem has become very heavy. We roll him in an office chair from the parking place to the front door. Erik pushes, I lift the leg.

As soon as Willem is lying on the sofa, the telephone starts ringing. I hear him talking: "In two weeks a walking cast, and then a brace. I'll go to school as usual."

But taking a crap is a problem. We lift our eighteen-year-old son to the toilet and the three of us get stuck in the small room. A chair on which to place the leg. The door can't be closed. Dependence.

At night we crawl next to each other. A sick child, a feeling from years ago. We've put a mattress in the room with a stack of pillows on it for Willem. The leg has to be kept high. Sara stays with her brother. He has a vase to pee in.

Pain. No appetite. Television. Having to ask for everything.

Before I go to work I place warm water, towels and toilet articles on the floor. I drive by the school to take homework and to pick up assignments.

"My leg is getting thin, I haven't any muscles."

"As long as it doesn't turn white, red, or black it says here in the folder. Or blue."

"My muscles are disappearing, just look!"

After a week the cast is loose. We go to the outpatient clinic for a check-up.

"What are you here for?" asks the clinic nurse. Although it's mid-winter, she isn't wearing stockings.

"Shouldn't you go for an X-ray first?"

"Go ahead," I say.

I drag the gurney through the halls. Wait. Back with the X-rays. Wait again. We read *People, Story,* and *Weekend.* We are called and are allowed to continue waiting in a narrow hall. Instead of a doctor, a brisk castmaster receives us.

"A walking cast?" Willem asks optimistically.

That's out of the question. The heavy plaster is sawn in two; they lift off the top like a lid from a bowl. Willem may choose the colour of the new plaster; the room is full of orange, blue, and yellow rolls. He wants black and white, the team colours.

"Shouldn't a doctor look at it?" I ask timidly.

"Next time," say the princes of plaster.

I shampoo Willem's hair in the kitchen sink and rinse it out with a saucepan. Every evening Dirk drops in for a while. They smoke together, and I disappear upstairs. In the cast room there were enormous condoms on sale, for pulling over the plaster so that you're able to take a shower without trouble. Willem isn't allowed to stand up. And the shower is upstairs. When I come downstairs in the morning, he's asleep on his back, next to the vase filled with piss.

130

"That leg needs a little push," says the orthopaedic resident.

We already have an hour and a half's waiting time under our belt; have been to the X-ray department, in the hall have secretly looked at the new X-rays (the bone fragments are at an angle), have been snapped at by the nurse without stockings, and have actually been counting on a walking cast.

A stocky Spaniard with a cheerful face comes in. "Time to make the walking cast."

"That's impossible," says the resident, "the position is not good."

"Nonsense. It's all right." The castmaster slaps the photo on the light box.

"In Salamanca we did it like that, and in Davos. It's sure to turn out all right. He has to put his weight on it. Grows together. Is good." He takes the stretcher; we roll Willem to the cast room.

The resident follows behind. "I don't agree with this!"

The saw is already screeching. While the cast nurses build a new harness, the master and the resident go into the hall. I hear them talking heatedly to each other. What now?

Grim-faced, the castmaster comes back in. He picks up the saw and starts removing the new cast. "Know-it-all. Some people are know-it-alls."

"Why does it have to come off?" I ask.

No answer.

Willem has to sit at the edge of the table so that his leg hangs down. He trembles; he can't control his muscles.

A nurse with big eyes behind glasses throws his arm around Willem's shoulder. "You have to relax, just let it hang."

"It doesn't work, I can't hold it still!"

Willem's voice sounds strangely high. He's crying. I get up and go to the hall. I leave the door wide open. "Who has final responsibility for the treatment around here?"

Annoyed, the clinic nurse looks up from the stack of X-rays in brown paper. "Aren't you being helped?" she says.

"Yes, by someone new every time. I would like to know who is the boss, who is in charge."

"Doctor Buikhuis, he is the chief."

"Then I want to speak with Doctor Buikhuis now."

"That's not possible. He's busy, you know. You're not on his schedule."

In the narrow hall there is a row of chairs on which people are sitting. Some have a plastered leg stretched out in front of them, others lug their armored elbow in a sling. At the end of the hall are four doors from which doctors appear from time to time, beckoning to patients.

"I'll wait until he has a moment. We're not leaving until we've spoken to him."

The nurse, the resident, and the castmaster go into conclave. They disappear with Willem's thick file into one of the rooms. Willem is lifted onto a stretcher. "Would you go with him to X-ray, to have a photo made without the cast. And then come back here," says the nurse.

I sit in the hall next to the stretcher, the new X-rays on my lap.

"My leg sure is thin, isn't it, Mum?"

"That's because you're not using the muscles, that's normal. When you start training, they'll get sturdy again. They're still there, but they haven't been used."

Disheartened, he squeezes his weak thigh.

Suddenly a tall man in a white coat stands in front of us. We may come in. He pushes the X-rays against the light box and we look. "We can heal a break like this in two ways. It can be stabilized with a cast, as has been done until now. Or we can put a metal plate against it. Then you'll be done with it in a month."

"We've already been at it for three weeks," says Willem, "in emergency they didn't say anything about a plate. I don't want to be operated on."

"Well, there are risks. If the plate site becomes infected, then it might take two years. If you choose the cast, you can't play soccer again until next season; it simply takes longer."

"But can it heal? Will it be all right again?"

"It's borderline; there is a slight angulation, but it's still acceptable."

Plaster. To the groin.

"Go and put some weight on it," says the triumphant castmaster, "to the pain threshold!"

Into the wheelchair, into the elevator, drive the car to the entrance. Put Willem into it, crutches alongside, wheelchair returned, to the exit, card forgotten. A line of honking cars behind us; I scream wildly into the small grid of the exit post.

"You have to back up," says the metallic voice, "stamp your card and come back."

I put my hands in my lap. A man gets out of a car behind us and comes to take a look.

"Problems? Oh, I know you from the television! Can I help you?"

Grateful, gratefully I press the parking card into his hand. He runs to a machine and stamps the ticket. We drive off jerkily; saved, helped, and freed.

The room is filled with screaming boys. Cases of beer stand on the floor. I dump chips into the fruit bowl, filling it to the brim. Arend toasts Willem. The boys give a cheer.

"Who are we?"

"The Speedy-eleven."

"WHAT do we do?"

"WIN!"

"For WHOM?"

"For WILLEM!"

Cheering. Everywhere there are sports bags, sweaty shirts and soccer boots with clumps of earth. This afternoon they won the return match in spirit. In reality it was 4–4. "That fat one didn't know what to do!"

"We crushed them!"

"Speedy-eleven will never go under!"

"Did you tell them what happened with Willem?" I asked Joost.

"Yes, that guy asked for his address, said he'd write a card."

With felt-tip pens the team members write their names on the cast. Willem sits on the air cushion and doesn't say much. This week he has started the first part of his finals, in an empty classroom on the ground floor of the school because he couldn't get up the stairs to the auditorium. In the evening he pulled himself upstairs, his leg in the cast thumping behind him. From his room, hard rock music began to pound, just as before. He didn't even want to come downstairs for Ajax-Feyenoord.

He spends the Christmas vacation on another couch, in the rented farmhouse. He plays computer games and reads required books. When it doesn't freeze, we take a short walk; the crutches shine in the low sun. He wears a special black sandal on the foot with the cast. Showers are possible again, with the giant condom which is put on with difficulty. At every check-up in the hospital we buy a book with crossword puzzles. Well over two months after the break, the cast is replaced by a flesh-coloured, rock-hard corset. While it is warm and pliable, the cast room officials fold it around the calf where it becomes stiff within five minutes. The knee is free!

Willem sets to work on his weakened muscles. We buy a standard book of muscle-strengthening exercises, and from his room comes the rhythmic shuffle of gymnastic movements. We buy barbells. His chest swells. In front of the television he lifts his leg a hundred times.

Walk, place the sandal carefully on the ground, catch the weight with the crutches.

"With one crutch," says the Spanish prince of plaster. "It hurts a little at first, but it's good. Press the bones together, then they start to grow."

On the X-rays we see a whitish film grow slowly around the break. The pieces of bone have found each other and are linking up.

One crutch at home and one at school. Ride a bicycle!

"Look at my leg, Mum, is it getting thicker? It's no longer all mushy, right?"

The brace may now be taken off at night. At home Willem sometimes walks without crutches on the soft floor. We go unarmed to the last check-up. The crutches have been returned, and the brace is at home.

136   During the course of these four months, we have seen five different doctors. Today we are received by a sixth. He is a short, slightly older man with a hoarse voice.

"Is it all right now?" asks Willem.

The doctor reads the records. He pulls one X-ray after the other out of the thick folder.

"They're not in order. How can I make sense of it? I want to familiarize myself with this. You want me to read the case history, don't you?"

We are silent. We wait. Willem gets out his book of crosswords.

During the examination he proudly shows off his regained skills: walking, bending his knees, standing on his toes.

"You can't play any sports yet," says the short doctor, "you might make unexpected movements and that would be dangerous."

He pushes the latest X-rays against the light box and places a ruler with a hinge over the fracture site.

"It is angulated. I'm not at all happy with that. A varus angle is allowed to be four degrees at the most, and this one is ten."

"It *is* allowed!" says Willem. "Everyone said that it was good!"

I come to his aid: "Not one of your colleagues has ever said anything about it. We've had at least ten check-ups."

"I don't think it's good. I'm going to discuss it at the staff meeting. Please make an appointment for four months from now, then we'll consider it again."

"Damn. What a shitty mess. I'm *never* coming back here. Let him look at his own crooked legs sometime, the dope! Just look, I can do everything again with my leg!"

Yes, he can do everything. We are going to eat in the city to celebrate his recovery. Afterwards Willem will go to the café with his friends. For the first time he is again involved in tactical soccer deliberations.

"The goalkeeper is quitting. He's too afraid. I want

to be goalkeeper, just like I used to be. After the vacation I'm going to train again!"

The telephone.

"Doctor Buikhuis' secretary here. Could you come tomorrow? The doctor wants to discuss something with you."

If only I weren't home. If only I didn't have a telephone. If only I could say no.

We don't have to wait and are immediately shown into the examining room where the history of the break is hanging against the light boxes. Doctor Buikhuis juggles with the angled ruler.

"We have conferred about it once more, at the end of the journey, and you see, there is a bend in the leg. The break itself has healed beautifully. That's not the problem. And what happens next? The bone presses slightly obliquely on the ankle, and this joint isn't made for that."

He looks at Willem.

"You are going to have trouble with it. Like Marco van Basten. You have to use that ankle for another sixty years!"

"That bend, wasn't it there from the start?" says Erik, who has also come along. "Why did no one say anything about it?"

"You yourselves chose a conservative treatment. It was a borderline case; most of the time it turns out well. We have a proposal. We're going to operate. We'll leave the break as is, but we'll saw a wedge out of the bone in order to compensate for the angulation. We'll drive two steel pins through the leg, underneath and above the wedge. They'll be connected to each other on the outside with screws. They're marvellous, those external fixations. You can tighten them as much as you want. After four weeks the pins come out—in adults we do it without anaesthesia. By that time they're usually loose anyway. Then another four weeks or so, and you're done!"

Doctor Buikhuis has stood up and is walking through the room, talking enthusiastically. His eyes sparkle and he is flushed. He points out on Willem's leg where he wants to saw and where the pins will be driven in. He sits down again and opens his appointment book. I hear Erik and Willem breathe heavily, I cross my legs and lean against the desk, my head slightly tilted.

"You have explained it very clearly and graphically."

"Yes," says the doctor, "it's so wonderful what can be done. In such a fracture we usually drive a long pin from the knee through the bone right away. Fantastic!"

"It's taken us a bit by surprise. Willem is in the middle of his finals. We have to get a little used to the idea."

"Well, we do have to schedule the operation. How about right after the examination?"

"In view of the seriousness of the surgery, I would

like to think about it a little and perhaps have the opinion of another doctor."

"You are free to do so. That's possible. But I wouldn't hesitate too long, you shouldn't wait a year with this, that would be damaging."

"Could you say anything about the chances of damage? A percentage. Is there any literature?"

"Madam, it's not like that. You have heard our opinion, there is a proposal, the family is going to consider it. What do we arrange?"

"You'll hear from us," I say, dazed.

I receive the heavy file folder with the records that I am to leave at the reception. Before doing so, I pull out the recent X-rays and put them under my coat.

"It sounds very plausible," say our friends. "You should consider it seriously. It's a university hospital, they can really do a lot. And they see a lot."

"Maybe someone needs to do a research project," I counter. "Not too long ago I heard about a series of operations on a ten-year-old child; they sawed out the bone and put it back in upside down. They must be out of their minds."

Think about it, I do nothing else. Ad nauseam I see an opened leg in front of me, neatly shaven. The muscles are pulled apart with meat hooks so that the pale bone lies defenselessly visible. A big green man wearing welding goggles sets the saw into it. Discreet hissing. The operating nurse sucks away the splinters. In a corner of the room stands the cannon with the steel pins. Willem is unconscious, a bathing cap over his long hair, without glasses. The intubation tube shapes his mouth into a white o.

"I'll do it right now!" he says while running back and forth between the refrigerator and the table. "Then I'll be done with it by summer."

"But what about your final exam?" I hear my voice tremble.

"We have to be practical," says Erik. "That doctor thinks it's necessary. Is it rude to go to another one—is it even possible?"

I start calling. The son of a friend was treated by the Feyenoord orthopaedist. "He is *very* talented, he was able to lengthen each leg eight inches for Ed de Goey, and you can't see it at all! He'll be glad to look at the X-rays."

Call. Appointment with a snappish secretary, in three months. Right before the vacation, that surgeon will be tired of sawing and Willem will have a lucky escape, I think. What do I actually want? I don't want them to cut into healthy flesh. I don't want to feel guilty if he limps in ten years. I don't want to keep looking anxiously at his ankle. I don't want pins through my son's leg.

The weather changes, near the pond the medlar trees come into leaf. Grebes chase each other over and under the

141

water. "Just ran around the pond three times!" says Willem as he comes in, sweating. "And I got a seven for maths! This summer we're going to the Pyrenees with the whole team; we decided that last night. Isn't that great?"

"You shouldn't force your own preoccupations on him," says my girlfriend. "Does he think those steel bolts are scary or do you? He's eighteen, he has to decide himself. But then he has to be able to talk about it, with you."

What kind of talking, I think. Wouldn't it be better to go to the hospital than to the mountains, do I have to I say that to him? Or: postpone that operation until the fall, when you've just started your studies. You're walking so well now, but you have a time bomb in your leg that keeps ticking with every step; do you have any pain in your ankle, do you feel anything, does it feel different from your good leg?

"The Pyrenees? That's nice, Willem," I say, cowardly.

"You can call Verbeuk," says an older, thoughtful colleague when we sit next to each other at a meeting. "I have informed him, and he is willing to give you a second opinion, provided that Buikhuis knows about it."

A few weeks later we stand in a dark oak-panelled doctor's office. The doctor is wearing a dark grey three-piece suit under the starched, conspicuously white coat. We shake his well cared-for hand. He wears shoes with six pairs of eyelets. On his pointed nose sit thick glasses in a transparent, surprisingly pink frame.

"Please tell me what happened."

I tell the story. The man asks nothing, only listens and looks at the X-rays that I've brought with me. Then Willem has to take off his shoes in the examining room and Verbeuk gets up. He disappears through the door. I remain seated by his desk.

Suddenly the doctor sits across from me and looks at me through the pink-framed glasses.

"The human locomotor apparatus is extremely well designed. Orthopaedic surgeons are enthusiastic constructors. They are surgeons and they operate. That is their profession. And mine, too. A violinist has to play the violin. A horticulturalist has to prune. We have to be orthopaedic surgeons in a world where not everyone is an orthopaedic surgeon."

Willem moves around in the small side room and comes in.

"Are we going, Mum?"

"Flexible. The skeleton is flexible and behaves unpredictably. Sometimes it's difficult to live with the knowledge that we can predict so little. I wish you both all the best. Do take these with you."

He pushes the X-rays into my hand, we stand on the sidewalk, in the sun, we're going to eat a pastry, I have a

143

glass of wine in the middle of the day, we're going away, we go to Paris.

Wind in Brabant, Belgian wind, French wind blows into the car. Towards evening we smell the city. Oysters, bridges of grey stone, parks, the river.

The Saint-Germain stadium in Paris. By a miracle we have four tickets for the match against Barcelona. It couldn't be better! Under the plastic covering across from us sits Cruijff. Cruijff!!

The game is terrible. The Spanish are clumsy and slow against the swift, agile French. Cruijff gets agitated; we see him standing and gesticulating after the opponent's third goal. His muscled cheeks are contorted in an angry grimace.

A substitution. With a commanding sweep of his arm Cruijff sends a slender-built youth onto the field. The blond hair waves up and down when he runs to his place.

"Jordi," says Willem, "he's putting his son in!"

The boy slips like a goldfish through the hefty defenders towards the goalkeeper. The crowd whistles. Goalkeeper and attacker, their legs extended, slide into each other. The ball rolls into the right-hand corner; the Spanish players cheer.

The goalkeeper has risen to his feet, spitting, but the boy sits helplessly on the ground, his arms extended behind him. His father goes running towards him. Men with stretchers rush across the field; clumps of grass fly up. Fifty thousand people start screaming.

The cost of cooking

The first Tuesday of every month, just before five o'clock, the head of Garden and Grounds turns on the fountain because the board of directors is coming for a meeting. The nurses cycling home are surprised by the suddenly spurting stream of water, a festive rain over the lawn of the hospital, a waste of money that excludes them.

I have on occasion suggested to the appropriate person in charge that this feudal nonsense be stopped. It would save some money, too; every little bit helps me to balance the books at the end of the year. As far as I'm concerned, that pond with its fountain should be filled in; filthy ducks live in it, soiling the surrounding grass with their droppings. Such a water display in front of the main building may look impressive, but it is not appropriate to tempt fate at a psychiatric hospital.

In the fifteen years that I have worked here, five patients have drowned themselves in the pond. Yes. That's not many compared to the fifty who have thrown themselves in front of the train, but the railroad runs over other people's property; that's not our responsibility. When I spoke to the head physician about this problem during the last New Year's reception, he said that it was his decided impression that a considerable number of the residents owed their recovery to the pond. Was he making fun of me? Can a view of water make you feel better? I don't know; I'm not a doctor.

I like nothing better than looking at the entrance gate that is always open during the day. I'm happy that I work in the main building, although my room could be a little larger. I also don't like the fact that it has two doors; everyone thinks they can just come in with remarks about finance that are mostly of no use to me. Still, I prefer to be where I am rather than having to go farther onto the grounds. There the pace becomes slower and slower, people misunderstand each other or no longer understand anything at all. The doors are certainly locked there.

The board members park their cars just anywhere. Mine has been standing in its own spot since eight-thirty this morning. I don't know if someone else's car is parked there during the weekend. "Chief Fin. Adm." it says on the sign, that's only for me. I don't know if I should enter the large meeting room at exactly five o'clock. That was the agreed time, but no one is sitting at the enormous table yet. They are standing on the balcony, the members of the board, their coats unbuttoned, smoking a last cigar (we decided not to smoke indoors); they slap each other on the back at the coffee machine and have thrown their papers on the table haphazardly. The medical director is late.

Once a year I have to present, explain and defend the annual report at a meeting with the administration and the board. Today.

"Come in, Fred," shouts the director as he walks up and sees me standing near the door. I have not taken along my case with all the documents, only a piece of paper with notes and the plastic-bound annual report itself; I see copies lying all over the table. You can't show what you don't have with you; people should think about that more often. In a moment I will take my place behind my annual report, in the middle of one of the long sides of the table. But first the greetings. I shake hands with all the members of the board; if they are in conversation, I stand aside and wait for a moment, cough softly; as soon as I have made the whole round clockwise, I sit down in my seat.

"Glad you're here, Te Velde," says the chairman, "welcome. We'll proceed right now, I'm opening the meeting."

They rearrange their papers, the agenda, their reading glasses. With tired faces most are slouching in their chairs; they work all day long in their law courts, city councils and universities, and they are no longer young.

I sit up straight. I have nothing to fear but am somewhat tense anyway. Through the balcony doors I see the fountain. It's already growing dark. I'll get home later than usual. Will Lydia wait with dinner? This morning I saw a rolled roast in the refrigerator; I hope she has cooked it today. "Again ready on time. Interesting. A big job excellently handled." The chairman is speaking. He invites me to give an explanation of the annual financial report. I have prepared that; from my notes I report on the assets and liabilities, the current assets, floating capital. After this, the gentlemen may ask questions; that is always the worst moment. They have to oversee, and according to the rules they may examine everything, see everything, and talk with everyone. In practice, that doesn't really happen. From time to time the chairman telephones the director, that's all. The supervision is limited to commentary on pre-arranged items, like this one here, by me. They don't really understand, mostly they look at the differences between now and the year before and are shocked by a hundred thousand guilders more or less. Small items, such as training or day care, those they can imagine.

Now that the children no longer live at home, it takes us three days to finish such a roast.

Embarrassed, they look over the page with board costs. All those dinners and mileage allowances add up to a considerable sum; they don't think about that when they are living it up at our cost. They also receive the Class 1A

Christmas hamper, but that is concealed under "other forms of remuneration". I receive a 1C.

The director walks around the table with glasses and bottles. I don't like commotion and noise during my presentation. I also don't want gin while working; he knows that quite well and is standing behind me with a bottle of water. He is the only one who understands anything about the ingenious structure of my report. He places his hand on my shoulder for a moment. The financial expert on the board left last year in a dispute when, after a short discussion, the other members got rid of the Christian principles of the clinic. Without God's Word he did not want to continue and left in outrage, I was told. I breathed a sigh of relief when I heard. Free. A child can field the questions that I get now. How high the "reserve of acceptable costs" should be, why the "surveillance" item has increased so much, whether the energy costs can't come down in the long run. The discussion peters out; no one can think of any more questions.

149

"A final comment, Fred," says the chairman. "When I look under 'patient nutritional service', I see a considerable increase compared to last year. Can you tell us anything about that?" He empties his glass and asks the director to refill it. Meanwhile I reflect. Has he caught on or is it a coincidence?

The director winks at me and lifts the gin bottle into

the air behind the broad back of the chairman. A fine mess
this is, I have to pull his chestnuts out of the smoking fire.
It's his own fault, and the fault of these pains-in-the-neck
here at the table who just sat there nodding hypocritically
when the question of kitchen innovations was brought up,
more than a year ago. I'm never in favour of innovation
unless it's about scrapping things. The fact that in a hospital
eating is done at set times seems efficient to me for the
kitchen staff. The fact that everyone eats the same thing is
convenient for the dietitian. Always has been like that, nothing wrong with it, and yet they wanted to change it. Innovation. "The meal experience has to be re-created," was the
way they talked about it. That means non-stop cooking,
everything on demand, variable meal-times, orders that are
rushed across the wards, prompt delivery to neighbouring
institutions which can thus abolish their kitchens and give
us the money released from their catering funds. I shook
my head but it wasn't up to me to criticize the policy.
When the first financial statements became available, it was
different, then I did have a few comments. Both food costs
and staff costs had risen exorbitantly, and no one knew
why. The revamped outlook on nutrition was introduced
in the press with great fanfare, and the hospital was not
eager for negative publicity. Carefully the director sounded
out the department heads who spoke highly of the freedom
achieved. Finally meals could be served at normal times, the
patients were kept active and involved by the need to formulate their food requests, independence increased, respon-

sibility, and so forth. It all sounded like Sunshine House.

Meanwhile the costs kept increasing. An inspection of the kitchen and an analysis of the work force yielded nothing, except for some overtime bonuses. More was purchased, certainly, but it was eaten too, and storage was no problem with the new vacuum-packing technique. The increase in costs remained totally mysterious. Then I decided I'd better veil in mystery the places where these costs are to be found in the yearly report. The director knows that a part is hidden under "costs tied to existing buildings", another part under "general management costs", and the remainder under "non-specific costs". The project is called "unscheduled cooking", and that gave me the idea of separating expenses and bookkeeping entries from each other as well. I entered into an inevitable conspiracy with the management; we wanted no scandal, and for the time being, no supervision either.

The director tells them about the success of the project. He asks me to explain that the intended meal distribution to old people's homes and to institutions for the mentally handicapped in the vicinity has not yet been fully realized, hence the imbalance of the accounts. In half a year the cost picture will probably—no certainly—look quite different. The thoughts of the board are already elsewhere; I breathe again, and in conclusion I discuss the consequences of the new environmental legislation. Then they thank me and I'm sent away. In the half dark I hear the fountain splash, it is damp and foggy outside. As I get into my car I look at the steamed-up windows of the conference room.

The paths between the pavilions are deserted. Where does all that food go? Who eats it?

*   *

I can already smell the beef roast in the hall. Under the coat hooks lies a big sports bag that I don't recognize. From the attic comes an all too familiar sound: Biene's exasperating violin playing. I open the kitchen door.

"Well," I say to Lydia, "rolled roast, delicious."

She stands pricking the meat with her back to me. I should say her narrow back. Formerly I saw 42 or even 44 in her clothes, but when I hung some of her clothes in the closet not too long ago, it struck me that there was no label larger than 38. When did that happen, this decrease in volume? And why? Did she want it herself or does it just happen like that at her age?

"Roemer is home," she says, still without looking at me. "We're all eating together."

"But it isn't Sunday. Why did he come?"

"He was in the area. Getting acquainted at a place for an internship, something like that."

"A rotation, you mean." Roemer, our son, studies medicine. Because his studies are a hard grind, and time-consuming, he comes home to eat only on Sunday after-noons. I think children should become independent. Roemer is twenty-five. At that age I was already an adult and had my first job.

"How was it today?" asks Lydia. I think you should keep your private life and your work separate. At home I seldom talk about what happens at work. There isn't much to tell anyway, it's the same every day.

"There was a meeting. They approved the annual report."

"Oh. Shouldn't we drink wine with dinner then? You must be happy."

Now I have to blush suddenly. If she knew about the unlinked cooking and my suppressing the secret costs, would she talk like that? Fortunately she doesn't look at me, I leave the kitchen and at the bottom of the staircase I stand listening to Biene. My daughter, the twenty-one-year-old apple of my eye, my scowling string player. From the time she was six, when she got her first violin, she has increasingly isolated herself. She tells us how she feels through her playing. Seven hours a day we hear her bow exercises, scales, chords. Then she storms down the stairs, slams the front door behind her and cycles away with the violin on her back. The rain strikes her pointed face. Sometimes I think that she should do something about her eyes, which look so dull; Lydia should know what to do about that. Now she plays long, lingering notes that blend into each other. She has to stand in the middle of the attic, otherwise she hits the walls with her bow. It's been a long time since I was upstairs in her room.

My son sits in the living room, on *my* chair, with *my* paper. Unlike his sister, he has a broad, open face and lively eyes.

He jumps up and starts putting plates on the table. I take the paper. Hurrying, Biene enters the room. Her hair is pulled back tightly in a pony tail. She rubs her long fingers against each other.

"Why are we eating so late? Where's Mum? It's nearly time for me to leave."

"Hello, Bien," says Roemer, "did you see my new bag, isn't it beautiful? If you go and live by yourself, then you'll never have to wait for meals again, do you know that?"

She looks at him scornfully. "I would like nothing better. If you find a house for me where I can practise all day long, I'll leave now."

I unfold the paper. Of course she's right, she's old enough to leave. But that she wants to as well, that hurts. She lacks nothing here. He eggs her on with his medical opinions.

"It's not healthy to have that violin under your chin all day long. You should take care of that spot, the tissue degenerates, you'll end up getting cancer. Art cancer."

Peering past the paper, I see that he comes up to her and with two fingers strokes the purple swelling on Biene's neck. She knocks away his hand and pulls up her collar.

"And then you'll go and cut into it. Hero!"

Clattering of cutlery and glasses. They're sitting down.

He talks about his study: finished with internal medicine, starting psychiatry.

"I'm going to work at your place, Dad. I was at the hospital this afternoon. The instructor asked if I was related to you. He knows you."

Yes. I take care of his salary and his instructor's budget. And as thanks he betrays me by sneaking in my son. Roemer has been at the back of the grounds, near the locked wards from which it's wiser to stay far away. He seeks it out. My hospital. Where is she with the food? It's so quiet in the kitchen. I get up.

Dazed, she is sitting on the kitchen chair and looks surprised when I enter.

"Roemer is going to do his psychiatric rotation in my hospital, did you know that?"

"No. Nice."

"I don't think so. It's much too hard for such a boy. All those patients who jump in front of trains and walk around screaming all day long—I think it's nonsense to confront a child with that."

"It's part of his study, Fred. If he doesn't do it there, he'll do it somewhere else. And it isn't that bad, is it?"

Why does she say that? She must have encouraged him: do it at Dad's hospital, then you can come and eat at home often.

"Isn't dinner ready yet? We're sitting at the table."

The roast is small and has turned almost black. Mashed potatoes. Salad.

"You still have to make sauce for the meat." She looks at me, nods, scrapes with a fork over the bottom of the pan. You have to tell everyone everything here, otherwise nothing gets done. When she was still working, she wasn't so absent.

Yes, she was absent, but in the sense of: not at home. During the day I didn't notice it because the library is open during office hours. On Thursday evenings she was always out, and she often organized lectures and discussion pro-grammes in the evening hours. Then she would come home with stories about the writers she had hosted, what they said, wore, drank, did. It irritated me then. Now I've changed my mind. I would be happy if she could be enthusiastic about a book or felt like meeting a writer.

The children stop talking abruptly when we carry in the bowls and pans. What were you talking about, I want to ask, but when I open my mouth I inquire about Biene's activities.

"Performance evening," she says, "no big deal, études."

Roemer cuts the meat. He has to use force. I pass the mashed potatoes. We eat. Biene takes a few hurried bites, then crumples her napkin and puts it next to her plate. My son and I make a well in the mashed potatoes which we then fill with gravy. Full men's plates. Lydia strokes the knife with her fingers. She empties her glass. Biene is already half-way out of her chair, facing the door, when Lydia suddenly starts talking. The rolled beef roast is hard and bitter. I cut the meat into small pieces that I mix with the mashed potatoes.

"I have decided something," says Lydia. Biene sits back down, on the edge of her chair. With her hand she feels her neck, touches the calloused spot, looks at her half-full plate. Roemer raises his head and looks at his mother. I continue eating, in silence.

Then we all continue eating. The moment blows over. With the fingers of her left hand Biene drums on her right forearm. She kicks impatiently against the table leg. Roemer wipes his mouth.

"Actually, there should be internships for every kind of training. You should be able to tag along with some top violinist, then you can see what the work is really like. And playing in a real orchestra. Next week I'll just see how they do it, a psychiatric hospitalization, for example. After a while you try it yourself, that's how you find out if you like it."

"You don't know what you're talking about," sniffs Biene. "Practising, that's my work. If you practise well, you can do everything, and you don't have to walk like a dog behind its master. Or let yourself be bossed around, like you."

"But it does give you cancer of the neck. And who's happy then that a doctor is around? You should think more carefully, you, but they don't teach you that at your school."

"Just because you're so perfect and know everything better, you still don't have to lecture me. Just make sure that all these stupid professors are satisfied with you. Stay out of my business!"

"I thought—" says Lydia.

Shall I take another piece of rolled roast? I'll just do it. Nothing is so awful as left-over food. The end piece. Completely black. Maybe I can cut off the worst. She is talking.

"About guests. It always used to be pleasant at the table. And many people miss that. They also say that you can give money for food in Africa. Or for the Salvation Army's Christmas dinner. But I mean inviting someone here. For dinner, just once. It's a good idea."

What is she getting at? Biene sits still; Roemer pushes his chair back.

"I found it in the *Hospital Newsletter* when I was cleaning your room."

She is talking to me. With the dull dinner knife I saw at the burned edges of the rolled roast. I never leave the *Hospital Newsletter* lying on my desk, I toss it right away into the wastepaper basket in my study. What is she doing in there? And finding in there?

"It was for patients who have been hospitalized for a very long time and who have no family. They asked the heads of the wards who would be suitable. For guest dinners. Then you could call a lady, the number was right there."

I forget to chew. Did Lydia call the hospital without discussing it with me?

"It was the other way around, of course, my telephoning; I'm not the head of a ward, but I wanted to be a hostess. When she understood that, it was all right."

"Did you give your name?" I ask hoarsely. "Did they know who you were? That you were my wife?"

"I don't know," she says. "Of course she wrote down my name. The guest is coming on Sunday. For dinner in the family circle, she said. There is a telephone number in case it doesn't work out, then they'll come a little earlier with a taxi. Well, now you know."

It's extremely unpleasant to eat at irregular times. Six-thirty is a good time, but then every day, it's the regularity that counts. The fact that we're so late today is because of me, but still it's her fault. She could have eaten with the children at the usual time. I'm not dying for dinner-table conversation after all that drivel at the meeting.

"Is it a man or a woman who is coming?" Biene has stood up and is buttoning her sweater.

"Maybe even a child, someone your age," says Roemer. "Schizophrenia manifests itself commonly in adolescence. Growing to maturity and separation from the parental home are stress factors that increase the psychic load enormously. With weakened capacity, decompensation is then obvious. Joke!"

Her face tense, Biene goes into the hall. She pulls her

159

coat from the coat rack and then comes back in to strap on her violin.

"Separate yourself!" she hisses. "You are such a sad case, you could go just like that into *ER*. Show-off."

The front door bangs shut but still I'm afraid she's taking the lock off the bicycle with trembling hands. Cycling through the evening air should calm her down sufficiently to concentrate on her étude. She is the one who makes herself play well. She's such a perfectionist that it sometimes frightens me.

Lydia is still sitting behind her plate. She hasn't touched the food. Why doesn't she clear the table? We can save the rest of the mashed potatoes, nice to bake in the oven so it gets a crust, with bread crumbs and butter. Tomorrow.

"Mum," asks Roemer, "do you think it's a good idea? It seems to me it's a lot of work for you, cooking and then also entertaining such a difficult guest. You don't *have* to."

I stack the plates and carry them to the kitchen.

Why do they send that stupid paper to my home address; don't I have a mail box at work? Why does my daughter take everything seriously? Why does my son insist on going to work in my own hospital? Suppose he finds out? Maybe they'll gossip in the department, he'll overhear something, he'll start thinking, looking for papers, find evidence. Oh, nonsense. I'm rattling on. I stop for a moment at the door, which is ajar. I hear them talking.

"Are you all right?" Roemer's dark voice. "You don't look too well, very tired. Are you sleeping well?"

"I thought: it's a distraction. And such a person would surely like to leave the grounds sometimes. It's for people who have been living there for years, permanent patients, what's it called?"

"Chronic," says Roemer, "chronic. It never gets better, they never come out of it. It means not acute. But nowadays they're doing a lot for these people. They are helped to become independent and live in houses in the city. The nurses then come and visit. This eating idea probably has something to do with it. I hope you won't overtax yourself. Can I do some laundry? I'll pick it up again on Sunday. I have to have my white coats clean and ironed before I start on Monday."

"Do you really have to wear a white coat there? How strange for a psychiatrist."

161

I hear Roemer getting up and I open the door. With his dark hair he must look great in a doctor's coat. The director never wears a coat. When I see people walking around in white, it's usually kitchen staff. Commodity guzzlers, overtime specialists, unschedulers! I take the dish with mashed potatoes and carefully transfer the rest to a plastic container. First let it cool, then into the refrigerator.

* *

At eight-thirty prompt I park the car between the lines of my own parking place. The director's station wagon is already there. Next to his Volvo, in the space for important guests, stands a passenger car with a business logo on it: "Bierdrager and Brink, waste treatment".

Last night I lay awake until I heard Biene come home. I listened for her to double-lock the door. For a long, a very long time she remained sitting in the living room. Maybe she was reading the paper on the couch, maybe she was watching a late-night show on television, maybe she was quietly sitting and waiting for me to come down and ask her how she had played. Lydia was breathing lightly next to me; I couldn't tell if she was asleep. I wanted to get up, carefully slide out of bed, but I didn't. The night is for sleeping. I wish it were different, that I acted before thinking, but it isn't like that. I lay awake until I heard Biene go softly up to her attic. I should have taken her to the music school as I used to do on performance nights, I should have sat in the audience to hear her étude. She should have asked. I should have suggested it. But neither of us did that. In order to fall asleep I imagined myself totally paralysed. Movement was inconceivable and nothing at all happened.

Mrs Kuilboer of Accounting always knocks on the door, but she opens it at the same time. I would like to say something about it, but because I greatly appreciate her orderly way of working I don't want to antagonize her. I like working with her; she understands how I think. She brings me a cup of coffee, as usual.

"Anything special today, Ans?" We call each other by our first names when we are by ourselves.

"There's something wrong with the waste treatment accounts. Early this morning I looked up the file for management. We'll be hearing about it. For the rest there's nothing. How did it go yesterday?"

For a moment I think she's asking about our dinner, and I feel an undesirable tension around my lips, as if, stuttering, I were going to tell about the burned rolled roast. She is referring to the meeting, of course. I rub my face and give a report. A censored report, because you should not place unsolved problems before a subordinate; then you avoid responsibility and undermine your own authority. Or does she know more than she lets on? I pull the stack of mail towards me; I want to start. Ans Kuilboer goes back to her office. I feel a strong urge to tell her that there is danger, that unscheduled cooking is getting out of hand, that it's become impossible for us to oversee what is happening. I want to take her into my confidence and ask for help. I would be crazy if I did that. She must be able to count on the fact that I have a handle on the situation. Just imagine.

At ten o'clock the director calls. He asks if I can come to his office for a moment. His room is on the ground floor, facing the garden. A spacious, light room with not much in it. The large desk is empty. In the corner near the window stands an exercise bicycle. A sports-loving, business-like atmosphere, you could say. It stinks of old cigar smoke, but there is no ashtray to be seen.

"Bierdrager was here," says the director. "I looked once more at those kitchen-related invoices that you pulled together for me. We have to figure it out, and soon."

Ans, I think. Ans gathered the invoices. Of course I'm responsible; if mistakes are made, I will be blamed.

"These large kitchen invoices are not the the most transparent," the director continues. "But bills from the kitchen waste collector, those I can still grasp. 'Removal of organic waste', it says on them, specified in gallons per month. He collects what is thrown away in the canteen, in the main kitchen and the department kitchens, and for this we pay him a fixed sum per gallon."

And Bierdrager resells it to hog farmers and cattle feed companies, I think. It used to be that you *got* money from the kitchen waste collector, or am I wrong?

The director bends towards me across the desk.

"Fred, you won't believe it! These invoices have become enormously high the last few months, eight to ten times larger than before. I had him come here, Bierdrager. I thought: he has new rates, or a new, crafty administrator— something has to be wrong somewhere."

Something is wrong with us here, I think. At any rate I should have noticed these higher invoices. Formerly that certainly would have happened, I have a nose for such things, I notice when something changes, no matter where. I'm getting old. I'm not watchful enough. I haven't been at my best these last few months. All the more reason to be alert now. Listen!

"Nothing at all has changed in his company. He simply picks up a great deal more from us. He even had to purchase a larger truck for it! Do you see what I'm getting at?"

I get it. Unscheduled cooking results in more waste. More food is purchased than is prepared or eaten.

"More food is thrown away since we started the unlinked cooking?" I ask. "How can that be since the number of patients has remained the same?"

Maybe they eat less. He can have them weighed, perhaps by the interns. But they also purchase more, I know that from Kuilboer.

"So they cook more than is needed," I conclude. "Waste, that's it."

"I fear that's true," says the director. "How it comes about I don't yet know, but we'll get to the bottom of it. I thought I should warn you, then you're abreast of the latest news. You managed to carry it off very well yesterday. They continued making kitchen jokes all evening long during dinner; the atmosphere was good and no one is worried, exactly as we wanted. That's it."

Slowly I walk back to my room, up the stairs, through the hall, past the secretaries' offices and the toilets. Once inside, I close all the doors and I sit down behind my table with my head in my hands. I force myself to think before I do anything. I should call Biene, ask how her performance went. What if I get Lydia on the phone? That will only cause anxiety, better not. I'll hear it this evening. Right now I'm here. I have slipped up, and now I have to fix it. Myself. Not sit and wait until management winds up its investigation. I'll go and investigate. Now.

Resolutely I get up and walk into Ans Kuilboer's office.

"Are these invoices of Bierdrager itemized according to collection point?" I ask while I remain standing in front of her desk. She interrupts her work, gets up, and closes the door to the secretaries' offices.

"I took the file in question to the director's office this morning; therefore I can't show it to you, but the invoices are according to date, not according to place. You can see on them how much he takes away per week, but not whether the waste comes from the kitchen or the canteen. Are there problems? You shouldn't have to pay attention to something as minor as waste disposal, or did you get an official order?"

She heard me go downstairs, of course, she always knows everything. What bad luck that Bierdrager doesn't invoice more clearly. Couldn't I just call the kitchen? But if something is fishy, it's easier for them to lie to you on the telephone, maybe. I'd better go over there. If need be, round the back; the kitchen complex faces the street, just like the main building. That way I don't have to cross the hospital grounds and I won't meet anyone. The director said nothing about Roemer. Strange.

"No, nothing special," I say. "Routine check. Thank you, Ans."

Self-reliance is of crucial importance. Think for yourself, observe for yourself, check for yourself. On the spot.

The footpath runs parallel to the freeway at a distance of about thirty feet, between two rows of stately old beech trees. The rain has made their trunks shiny and smooth, like wet rubber. I walk over millions of withered beech leaves past the gates of the hospital. How often I used to walk through such woods with the children, looking for chestnuts, beech-nuts, and boletus. Lydia and I would sit smoking on a fallen tree trunk; we still smoked then. Roemer and Biene played store or restaurant with their harvest. A plate of fresh acorns, please, waiter. Do you want some moss with it, madam? Waiter, it's dirty. You do have to finish your plate, madam. Lydia cut through the boletus with her pocket knife and threw away the wormy ones. When Biene had to pee, Lydia held her legs, and the stream would splash against the beech tree. Roemer hid amidst the rhododendrons and barked like a fox. I carried a sack filled with sandwiches, cake, bananas, apple juice. It smelled so like autumn, like what autumn is. Just like here.

My shoes are getting messed up.

The trees break up the sound of cars rushing past into Morse code.

I'll have to do it myself. If I do nothing, she won't get away, she can't do it any more. I have to help her. I'll go to her this evening, up two staircases. Sign up for the Conservatory housing, I'll say. You have to. If you're lucky, within a few months you'll get a room where you can play day and night, in a house where young people are living, where you can go in and out freely, where it's normal, maybe even nice.

I'll help her move. The music books in a box, the clothes. We'll carry everything downstairs, out of the house.

Now that I've made this decision, I walk faster. Smoke and steam fan out of the small metal pipes on the roof of the kitchen building. I pull open the door with force. In the entrance hall there is a wall of smells that makes me recoil. Boiling fat, fried onions, sickly smelling carrots, a hint of fish odour; the mixture of suffocating food vapours almost makes me gag. The door of the office stands open, but the room is empty. I step into the room leading to the area of the kitchen ranges. The kitchen noises keep increasing; there is sizzling, ticking, cracking. Spoons bang against metal, knives on hard wood. Next to the giant kitchen island stands the Head of Nutrition. He is looking over the shoulder of a young man dressed in white at a baking sheet carpeted in sausages. He doesn't see me. I cough but the sound is lost in the din. I come closer and feel the heat radiate from the wall of oven ranges. The young man has tied a checked apron around his waist. He wipes his hands on it and walks away. My hand extended, I walk towards the chief. He looks surprised but not unfriendly.

"Well, are you coming to take a look, Te Velde? You should have changed your shoes, you're not really allowed to come in with outdoor shoes."

I look down. He is wearing white clogs with rubber soles. Beech leaves are sticking to my black oxfords. I apologize. To the point. Does he like unscheduled cooking, how many additional staff does it require, and, most important, how much more food is left over.

"Better than expected, Te Velde, much better than expected. I was afraid of that too, at first. But we've got the sealing process, you know, that's been our salvation!"

I don't understand him, and he shows it to me. Immediately after preparation, the ready-to-eat dishes are packed in transparent plastic which is then vacuum packed and heat sealed. The packages, labelled according to date and contents, are stored in the cool space on the other side of the building.

"It also saves on overtime. The cooks can do their work during their usual hours, and we save the food until there is a call for it. A great invention, you don't taste any difference from the fresh. And no spoilage because the air is out. You can, so to speak, keep everything for eternity exactly as it was at its best. Therefore we don't have much more waste than formerly, no. We do have more in stock now, but that will even out. I think the project is a real challenge."

How quiet it will be. How intensely I will long for the slow fragments from the *Chaconne*. How I will crave the empty fifths that precede everything: the a, the a and the d, the d and the g, dangerous depth, and then finally the triumph of the high e.

A shiver makes me take a step closer to the range. I stare at the sheet of plastic in the hands of the chief.

Sneak up to the attic. Push the plastic wrapper over her, carefully, in order not to wake her. Fit the tip to the pump and then pump, sweating with all my strength quickly remove the air of the present. If she should wake with a start, she would no longer be able to move; the tough, transparent material sticks to her legs and her stomach, it pushes shut her eyelids and it closes on her narrow mouth. It sticks against her pointed nose and covers the wound on her neck. Seal shut. Eternity.

Am I fainting? I grasp something, I grope for the red-hot baking sheet. I don't remove my hand until I can distinguish the piercing pain from the pleasant feeling of smoothness, from the strange sensation caused by an unusual temperature. It feels as if I press ice in my hand, but I smell scorched flesh.

A man screams.

In the office a nurse comes with gauze and bandages. She disinfects the wounds and smears ointment on it with a glass spatula. Shaken, the Head of Nutrition stands aside.

"Its stuffy in there," he says. "We should have a new ventilation system; the old one is inadequate now that we are cooking all day. I'm going to see to it. Are you in much pain, Te Velde? I would take a bunch of painkillers if I were you, burns are nasty."

He takes me to the door, apologizing profusely. No waste. I know enough. In my hands nags a pleasant pain.

*   *

On Sunday morning I wake from a very deep sleep. Right away I start sorting out my thoughts. I should not cast vigilance aside to that extent: the curtains were pushed open without my noticing it. The window is a light grey surface over which a branch of the ash tree sweeps from time to time. I feel the palms of my hands; the wounds pull. On the chair next to the bed stands a box of see-through plastic gloves, a present from the management.

"For when you go to the toilet," said the director, "or do something else which might get your hands wet or dirty. You don't need an infection as well." Plastic over skin, I suppress a shiver. It is a practical present that I can certainly use; gratitude suits me. Friday, right before closing time, Biene bicycled to the student advisor. I haven't seen her since then; she has a rehearsal weekend with the conservatory orchestra. Roemer did come home yesterday. I heard him confer with Lydia in the kitchen. Lydia—is she up already? The bed is empty, her clothes are gone. I sat with the newspaper in my damaged hands and listened to the conversation between mother and son. They didn't talk about Roemer's first week in admissions but about Sunday's menu.

"Pork with Prozac," said Roemer, "Hare in Haldol! You can't be too careful. Shall we go shopping together?"

Lydia giggled; she wanted to make something that she could prepare beforehand so that she'd have her hands free to receive the guest. The kitchen door banged shut. Through the window I saw them walking, Roemer with the shopping bags and Lydia with a piece of paper in her hand. They waved at me.

It wasn't until they had truly and finally disappeared that I folded up the paper and went upstairs. Two staircases. I crawled into my daughter's bed and lay there as long as I dared with closed eyes, my arms crossed on my chest.

With my hands wrapped up, sealed at the wrists with rubber bands, I can even wash my hair. Sunday is usually a terrible day, without routine and without fixed activities. I should be happy that I passed the morning unconscious, but I feel anxiety roaming in my stomach. Biene. The psychiatric patient. Lydia.

"Don't you want to call off that whole dinner?" I asked her last night. The wind shook the windows.

"The patient is counting on it, I don't want to disappoint her."

"It is not a disgrace if it's too much, that can happen to anyone. Call that lady tomorrow morning, then you're done with it." Silence. I smelled her sourish breath.

"Certainly not. It's no bother. Roemer will help me."

They sit together at the kitchen table, they peel the potatoes, they cut the vegetables. Bowls, knives, cutting boards. On the corner of the kitchen countertop I see a stack of dishes, five glasses, cutlery. Everything is in order, that does me good.

"I think the atmosphere is pleasant," says Roemer. "The department head is just plain nice. It is much calmer than I expected; I can talk for hours with the patient to get his anamnesis. Dad, what would you think if I became a psychiatrist?"

I pour myself some tea but then stop in the doorway.

"If you want to," I say. "Do wait, there will be other rotations. Didn't you want to be a surgeon? Psychiatry, I don't know. It doesn't mean much to me; I only deal with the money there, for me it's a business."

Without spilling, Roemer stirs oil and vinegar in a water glass to make salad dressing. He has surgeon's hands: large, muscled, well cared-for. Lydia peels a potato. She drops it into the pan which is in her lap. Water splashes.

"The meat," she says, "what time should the meat go into the oven?'

"I'll do that." Roemer pulls the casserole from the refrigerator. In it lies a purple lamb roast, bathing in red wine with garlic cloves. I can't look at it. If only it were Monday.

In my study I collect all the data about unscheduled cooking. Because I always save everything, I can compare it with the summaries of the situation before the experiment. What has changed, how is that change reflected in the aggregate of income and expenses, why can't the leak be localized? I don't manage to think clearly and I sweep the papers together into my briefcase. Tomorrow, at work.

In the kitchen it now smells of roasted meat. There is steam on the windows. Roemer leans against the kitchen countertop with a glass of wine in his hand, and Lydia is stringing beans even though nowadays they no longer have strings. A strand of hair hangs over her face; it makes her look young. What are they talking about? It's not getting through to me. A family, I think, a family in a warm kitchen where everyone has known all the objects for years. The enamelled colander, the salad bowl of heavy, Finnish glass, the orange soup pot. The son hands the father a glass of wine; the mother lowers the hand with the paring knife into her lap. My eyes are wide open; if I remain staring like that at my family, without blinking, my corneas will dry up, and I will see them, the mother and the son, until I no longer see anything.

The kitchen door flies open and a cold gust of wind pushes the daughter inside. Her hair is windblown and her cheeks are flushed. She is smiling. She raises her hands in the large winter mittens triumphantly; she jumps in the air; she shouts with joy: "I have a house already! Next month. That Korean violinist is suddenly going back, and now I can have his room, I just heard it." She starts and claps her hands over her mouth.

Oh Biene, father and mother's daughter. You had meant to be careful, silent. First confer with me, or before that, take Roemer into your confidence. Then wait for an appropriate moment for the next announcement. Too late. I see her wince and with trembling mouth look at Lydia.

"What are you doing?" she asks in a small voice. "Oh, for that guest. Of course. How *stupid* of me!"

Roemer wants to say something but doesn't get further than a gasp for breath. He too looks at the thin woman at the table. I have raised my arms as if to catch a victim from a burning house and hold my breath.

"How wonderful for you, dear," says Lydia. "It's great that it worked out. Congratulations!" She stands up, she gives Biene a kiss. No one says anything; I hear the lamb sizzle and the potato water boil. Family scene: mother kisses daughter, father and son watch. Don't move. Photo-op!

A car stops in front of the house; the doorbell rings.

Then there is a storm of movements, footsteps and doors flying open. I'm still standing in the kitchen in a daze when a small woman enters the hall. Lydia has shaken her hand, said "welcome" to her. The woman is wearing a light raincoat. She stands stock-still on the doormat and looks at us from behind enormous glasses that magnify her eyes. The skin of her face is furrowed and wrinkled, the curly grey hair looks just-shampooed. No one moves.

"Come, I'll help you out of your coat," says Lydia finally. "Then I'll introduce you to my husband and my children. I didn't catch your name, could you say it once more?" Accompanied by Lydia's words, the woman takes off her coat. She is wearing a dark wool dress with long sleeves. In good taste, it seems to me. On her feet are checked slippers. Quickly I turn my eyes away.

"Mrs Onstenk. Call me Annie." The voice is unexpectedly strong and deep. I come forward to greet her. Is she allowed to drink wine or will she get out of control; it might not react well with her medication; Roemer should say something; what should be done? Before my fumbling becomes blatant, Lydia has taken her to the living room, and Roemer offers a glass of water. We all sit down. There should be music. If only Biene would practise; she went upstairs. Shall I ask her for some Bach?

Roemer starts taking her history. Mrs Onstenk answers all the questions without hesitation. She is forty-six years old, which I consider very young, having taken her for older when she was standing in the hall; she is no longer married and has no children; she has been living in De Bosrand, which I know is a ward for chronic patients, and formerly worked for the postal service. After every answer she waits with arms crossed for what will come next.

"That I don't remember anymore," she says when Roemer asks how she landed in the hospital. "Next question."

"What do you enjoy," asks Lydia, "what do you like to eat?"

Just when Mrs Onstenk is about to answer, Biene comes into the room. She has changed; she has put on a black skirt and a shiny blouse, and shoes with high heels.

"I'm Biene. You've come to eat with us. I'm going to set the table." With us, she says. I'm proud of her.

"We have no first course," says Lydia, "there is dessert. I hope you like lamb?"

While the children prepare the table, Mrs Onstenk sits down. I sit down across from her. She looks at the bandages on my hands.

"You're from the home too. I've seen you."

Lydia carries in the lamb. "My husband works there. He's not a doctor, but he manages the administration; you probably know him from there."

Now we are all sitting around the table. Roemer gives everyone a helping of meat and Biene pushes the dishes with beans and potatoes towards Mrs Onstenk. Two spoon-fuls, three, four. The plate is completely filled, the salad doesn't fit. I can't help watching how Mrs Onstenk shovels in her food. She doesn't spill anything, she keeps her mouth closed when she chews, she uses knife and fork. With great concentration and at high speed she eats everything. I can't keep my eyes off it. Lydia asks Biene about the room; they talk about dimensions, curtains, kitchenware. I watch the wrinkled cheeks where the meat is being chewed. This woman has an intense interest in food.

"How is the food on your ward?" I ask. "Are you satisfied with it?"

"It's good," says Mrs Onstenk with a rasping voice. "We used to have dinner at midday, then the food cart would sometimes come as early as noon and you'd have to be ready. But now it's in the evening. Soup, croquettes, all sorts of food, and always dessert. Cake or pie or grapes or pancakes. It's a lot of work because you have to fill in the lists, to mark what you want to have. That's what they bring."

"Is that difficult, those lists? Do they help you with them?"

"If they have time. It's very difficult. Everything is mixed up. You have to know what there is and what you feel like eating."

I have put down my knife and fork. I turn towards her.

"Could I perhaps see such a list?"

Mrs Onstenk takes the canvas bag that is hanging on her chair and pulls several sheets out of it. She looks at them carefully, chooses one which she then hands to me, across the platter of lamb.

"Do you want something else to eat?" asks Roemer.

Mrs Onstenk takes a helping of salad. I take a quick glance at the order form. It is divided into five sections, each filled with possible choices. First courses, vegetables, main courses, side dishes, desserts. I hold the paper so tightly that my wounds pull.

"You *have* to mark something," says Mrs Onstenk. "If you mark nothing then you get *everything*. You have to learn that."

"How does it work?" Let her continue talking, don't interrupt her, don't distract her! Mrs Onstenk eats some salad. Her wrinkled jaws grind and grind. She swallows.

"Difficult," she says. "Mrs Pasman, she's too heavy. The doctor had said: no potatoes. She can only have the vegetables. But in the evening her food came and everything was on her tray."

I nod and read from the form. "Potato dishes: boiled, fried, mashed, French fries; potato substitutes: spaghetti, macaroni, white rice, brown rice."

"And Mr Moens never wants first courses because he says that takes away his appetite. Every day he gets chicken soup, tomato soup, coleslaw, Russian salad, shrimp croquette and egg roll."

Carefully I fold the form in four and stick it in my inside pocket. I lean back in my chair and sigh.

179

Mrs Onstenk spoons up her dessert, gets up, and sits down in front of the television. She is waiting for something. Her feet in slippers are placed next to each other on the floor. We do not yet leave the table or clear away, clean up, put water on for tea, brew coffee. The four of us sit silently at the table where we have sat for twenty years.

"When she had become thin, she left," comes from Mrs Onstenk's chair. Her grey curls stick out above the back of the chair. "That is unpleasant, sometimes someone leaves suddenly, then they go to live on their own, in the halfway house. We get cake with the coffee, and then the van comes. That's not nice."

Mrs Onstenk starts sobbing her heart out.

Everyone is asleep but I still sit at my desk. I'm writing a report about the failure of management in the unscheduled cooking project. Tomorrow I will give it to the director. Shall I also advise him against letting patients dine out like that, or is that going too far? I do have an opinion about it after this evening.

Mrs Onstenk was inconsolable. Roemer turned on the television, but even during *Studio Sport* the tears kept streaming down the deep wrinkles in her cheeks. Biene got water, a napkin, stroked her hands. It didn't help. Lydia who had remained at the table, as if petrified, finally looked up the emergency number and telephoned. Within fifteen minutes a taxi came to pick up our crying guest. I speak from experience.

I sign my name at the end of the report. I stretch and

walk into the kitchen. The kitchen countertop is spotless. Everything has been washed and cleared away; there is no trace of any commotion or confusion. Nothing is wrong; we have survived the evening; the mystery is solved; I can go to sleep.

*   *

Biene and Lydia are still asleep when I leave. Roemer has left long ago; he was expected on morning rounds at seven o'clock. It's cloudy and chilly. Rain. In my bag are the sheets of paper that I typed last night to hand to the director. I have added Mrs Onstenk's list of choices as appendix.

    "He isn't here this morning," says Ans Kuilboer. "He's at the Department of Health. I can ask his secretary to let you know when he returns. Do you want coffee?"

    I shake my head and walk back to my room. It's cold everywhere. That's because they turn off the heating in the main building over the weekend. When Biene has moved I can turn off the radiators in the attic. Savings in telephone costs can be expected. Food expenses will decrease. Though when Roemer left, Lydia cooked for four people for a long time. She couldn't get used to it. Shall I put my report on the director's desk? No. If he isn't here he won't get it. I'll take care of the mail.

The canteen stinks of tomato soup and wet coats. A nauseating vapour comes from the smoking area. I had my hands cared for by the male nurses at the first aid station. The wounds look good. They itch; that's a sign of healing. I finish the soup on the spot; the rolls I take with me to my room. I close the door to Ans Kuilboer's department; I leave the door to the hall open. I'm feeling short of breath. My report lies on the edge of my desk. Shall I have a nice cover put around it? No, it's not worth the effort. It should have been sent off a long time ago.

Unannounced, the director stands in the room. He still has his coat on and the rain drips from his hair. His face is tense from the cold.

"Good that you've come immediately," I say. "I have a lot to tell you. In my opinion, it's solved!" I stand up, pick up the report, and wave it back and forth in front of his face. "By constant alertness you can take advantage of a lucky coincidence. I'll explain everything."

He looks at me, not understanding.

"Do sit down, Fred."

"But I—do you have bad news from the Health Department?"

"No. Yes. Bad news. You haven't heard yet?"

Suddenly my hands hurt a lot. I lower myself into my desk chair. The director pulls another chair closer and sits down face to face with me. I put the report on my lap and hold it tight.

"Lydia is not doing well, Fred," says the director. "We had to admit her again."

"No, that can't be. She was very well yesterday. She cooked for a patient. You're mistaken."

"Thanks to that patient we were there in time. She tried to commit suicide again. With pills. We still don't know how she got hold of them. Did she get anything from your family doctor?"

"But yesterday—that lady was gone, wasn't she? This morning she was sleeping normally. The kitchen was cleaned up so beautifully. What?"

"Mrs Onstenk was very confused last night. She kept saying that she had forgotten to take along flowers for Lydia. This morning one of the attendants went with her to buy a bouquet of flowers and they took them to your house. No one answered. Jack, the attendant, wanted to leave again but Annie Onstenk suddenly ran to the back, to the kitchen door. She saw Lydia lying on the floor and started screaming."

Biene. Biene was home, wasn't she? Or had she already cycled off with her violin?

"No one was at home. We had to force open the door. The ambulance came quickly. Her stomach has been pumped. She is not yet conscious. Do you want a glass of water?"

Her stomach. She didn't eat much yesterday. I see Mrs Onstenk before me in her checked slippers in our wet garden, waving a bouquet of asters. Lydia was so nice to her. So controlled. So healthy.

"Are you all right?" asks the director. "You should come with me now, then you can see her. There's some administrative stuff that we have to take care of."

Mechanically I stand up and get my coat, I put the rolled-up report in my pocket. The director opens the door for me and lets me go ahead. I don't know which way we have to go. He takes me by the shoulder and guides me over the asphalt path, far into the grounds.

"There's another unpleasant matter," he says. "Your son. He appears to be doing his rotation here."

"He started last week. He likes it very much. He found it peaceful."

"Yes, that's not the problem. He's working in admissions; he was there when Lydia was brought in. That's impossible, of course. He was rather upset."

"Roemer is going to be a doctor," I say. "A surgeon. And my daughter Biene is training to be a violinist. She'll soon be leaving the house. The children are independent. Both of them work hard. That's nice for us to know. Often children don't turn out well. But we can't complain at all about our children, not at all. Quite the contrary."

"Here we are, Fred." The director sticks a key in the lock and the door swings open. I recoil. Here is where it was. Here I went every day to sit for half an hour across from someone who was silent. Silently we agreed to keep silent. I decided never to set foot in here again. I am pushed inside.

It looks different. The doors and the skirting boards are painted bright red, and the living room is smaller. "Renovation of existing structures" item: every patient must have a private room. Shatterproof glass in the windows and in the partitioning walls; those are "building-connected costs". At the back of the pavilion is the ward. A man lies snoring on a high bed. The director tells me to turn around. There is far too much light here; what a waste of energy for a room where nothing is done besides sleeping.

She is lying in the corner. An IV has been placed in the back of her hand. She is almost as pale as the pillow case. Her lips are cracked. Yesterday at this time she was stringing beans. A nurse comes to take her blood pressure and her pulse. She writes her findings on a paper in a dark blue plastic cover. Then she taps Lydia's cheek.

"Mrs Te Velde, wake up! Your husband is here!" From her voice I can hear that she doesn't hold out much hope.

The director has taken off his coat and takes me to a room or an office a little farther down the hall. I keep my coat on. I feel the rolled-up report in my inside pocket.

Roemer stands at the window with his hands in his pockets, without a white coat. He turns around. He has been crying.

If Biene would come and give a concert here, then the four of us would be together again, I think. Conservatory students have to practise performing, and for the patients it would be a welcome change. Some people say that music has a healing effect.

"Why did you never say anything," Roemer snarls at me. "Why the hell do I have to find that out here? A re-admission. They got out the old file. Another suicide attempt. I didn't know what they were talking about. My own mother."

"You weren't there. You had just moved out. I didn't want to burden you. She got better."

Roemer kicks against the desk. He walks past me to the door. My son, my little boy.

"Yes, I was living on my own, not even a month. And what happened yesterday? That nice announcement by my sister! You are so stupid, so short-sighted, so egotistical! Sort it out yourself. I'm leaving."

186 It goes on and on. Trembling, the large hand moves past the minutes. There is screaming in the hall, but I have closed the door. If someone isn't awake or is in a coma, he can't fill in the food list. Does he then get a tray with all available dishes or does he get nothing at all? I should research the processing of the menu requests more closely. How is it entered into the computer, with a scanner or by a stupid temp? A hospital is immensely more complicated than most people realize. Automatic processing; I bet on that, otherwise the mistake would have been discovered.

The director comes back. He carries a tray with two plastic cups of tea. Sugar bags and stirring sticks lie carelessly dumped next to them.

"Very difficult for you. A very unfortunate coincidence that your son was on duty. But understandable: it was urgent, she had to go to the closest hospital. And she was known here. As soon as she is conscious, we'll transfer her; I'm sure you agree with that? I have given Roemer the rest of the week off. Actually, it seems to me that it would be better for him to do his rotation somewhere else. I'll talk to him about it."

Slowly I stir the sugar through the tea. I really don't like these plastic cups. Too hot to hold, and they give warm drinks an unpleasant taste. I pull the report from my pocket and offer it to the director.

"Now that we're talking anyway," I say, "I can tell you that the mystery of unscheduled cooking has been solved. I traced a serious error in the data processing."

"Fred, shouldn't you take a few days off as well?"

"I still have to research the administrative support of the food service in more detail, that's where the error is. Within a week I'll be able to inform you in more detail. It is an extremely stupid system, I'm curious as to who introduced it."

"You have to go home, Fred, to your daughter. Can you drive or shall I have someone take you home?"

I stand up. "It would give me pleasure if you would accept this report from me. Please read it through carefully. It's unbelievable. It sheds a very unfavourable light on the quality control of the food service department. Wasteful. Incompetent. Scandalous. Disconcerting. Frightening. Sad. Desperate."

The director takes me by the hand carefully; he doesn't want to hurt me. He has taken the report with him. We go outside. The rain falls on our faces.

The man who loved disappointments

She had set aside a good hour for driving to Hilver-
sum, she said. The programme was to start at nine o'clock,
and a little past eight my friend was already on the city
beltway. Next to her on the empty seat lay a map of the
Gooi area, a street map, and the directions from the radio
station which had invited her. Because the sun was so low
she couldn't read the street signs, and soon she no longer
knew where she was. First she had calmly pulled the car
over to the side of the road, picked up her sunglasses from
the floor, and got her reading glasses from her purse. She
had tried to backtrack via a side road, but orange detour
signs led her to a deserted shopping centre that she couldn't

find on her map. Turning around was impossible, there was one-way traffic everywhere.

Then she had started to curse and sweat. The map got caught in the cord of her reading glasses. She pulled on it and broke off an arm of her glasses. The directions had slid onto the floor. Behind her people had honked impatiently. Fifty years old, she had thought, and still unable to find the way, even though at home she had studied the maps for a considerable time, gesturing in the air with right and left hands in order to imprint the directions firmly in her mind. She had been here before; she was a writer; she could think. Now, with tears in her eyes, she sat behind her steering wheel, pounding it powerlessly. Never again. From now on anyone who wanted to have her on a pro-gramme would have to pick her up and take her home afterwards. She had asked for directions at a petrol station and had been sent very kindly to the wrong radio station. From there it took another fifteen minutes of navigating around torn-up intersections to get to the right building.

The sun was setting. She took off her sunglasses, threw the reading glasses out of the window and turned off the ignition key. Breathe deeply and get out calmly, she had thought. Smooth your clothes and remember what it was about. Soccer. Tomorrow's game. She wondered if it was a live broadcast. She hoped not; in the distance a clock tower started to sound nine.

The parking lot lay at the foot of an enormous square, across which a man came running. He grabbed my friend's arm and pulled her to the entrance at a stiff pace, grumbling all the while that she was late. He continued holding on to her in the building while dragging her up and down stairs, running through dark hallways with empty seats, and jumping over thick bundles of black cables.

In the studio ablaze with light, people sat behind panels. It smelled of stale coffee. A red light was on above the door to the recording room. She was pushed inside; the man pointed to an empty chair behind the narrow, horseshoe-shaped table.

She sat down and placed her cigarettes in front of her. Philip Morris. At her left side the fat correspondent was grinning behind his Gauloises, at her right the former soccer player lit up a Marlboro. Red, white, and blue. The programme director looked at her reproachfully. He was busy giving an enthusiastic introduction and his glasses were already steamed up. A live broadcast, obviously. A spontaneous discussion about Soccer and Art. She took off her shoes under the table.

My friend recounted that the conversation did not get going easily, not even after the host had put on cheerful soccer music. The columnist knew nothing about soccer and snickered derisively when the host began talking about art. My friend can write, but her soccer knowledge consists primarily of the family background of the players. When she spoke entertainingly about the relationship between soccer

talent and family size (Van Vossen! Bogarde!) the host inter-
rupted her. That was not art. Wasn't soccer a form of dance?
The host pushed a button, and the studio was filled with
the voice of a famous ballet dancer speaking admiringly
about the rhythm and sense of pace of certain Ajax players.
The fat correspondent snickered. My friend felt an increasing heat on her right side. The former soccer player made
groaning noises and blew the smoke of his cigarette with a
hiss through his teeth. He looked fixedly at his clenched
fists that lay in front of him on the table. His hair hung
messily in front of his eyes.

She wondered whether she might be able to think of
something constructive about soccer as an art of movement.
Might there exist a choreography for soccer matches so that
you could rehearse a very successful match again in its
entirety? Almost all soccer players, just like dancers, started
giving lessons after turning thirty-five. And were there similarities, or instead differences, in sexual identity?

She didn't have to use her discussion topic because as
soon as the tape with the remarks about ballet was finished,
the former soccer player exploded. Total nonsense, all of it,
he roared. Why had they pulled him away from his fireside
to listen to this sort of nonsense? Locked up in this lousy
hole! He wanted out, he didn't want to participate, he'd
had it, totally. Disgusting, he'd said, dis-gust-ing. My friend
blushed slightly at the memory. He had a nice voice, she
thought.

An intense, suffocating silence had fallen in the room.

The host no longer knew what to say. On the back legs of his chair, the columnist leaned wobbling against the wall and hiccupped with soundless laughter. Seconds ticked past. In how many cars, kitchens, and mobile homes did surprised listeners start turning radio knobs and never again turn back to this station? Behind the window of the technical studio, she saw the bewildered faces of the recording staff. Quick as lightning, she had reflected: he was right, that former soccer player; she would like to dash outside with him to continue cursing; perhaps she could save the situation by pretending that they had just given a demonstration of the new sudden-death rule; she was imprisoned here with three silent men who for three different reasons would not speak again—in a live broadcast of a talk show.

Then she had turned to the soccer player and had asked him if he had actually missed soccer after his career had suddenly come to an end because of a serious injury. His head had come out of its bent, angry position. He had looked at her, twisting his mouth with its irregular teeth. Not for one moment, he had said. Never. Not at all. Then he had smiled almost shyly and had whispered that he loved disappointments.

My friend is also my neighbour. We were talking in the parking area behind our houses. It was a mild evening. We sat down on the bumpers of our cars that were parked next to each other and we smoked.

He hadn't been the usual flirt, said my friend when I raised my eyebrows at the end of her story. She didn't care for losers. She also didn't care for men who lost because they didn't know what to do with a victory. He had meant something else, something deeper, something important. It kept haunting her.

I was silent. She told me how it had ended, how everyone had stood in the hall rather self-consciously and slightly embarrassed and had then said good-bye. She had shaken the hands of the host and the columnist but had kissed the soccer player. Why? Body language, she thought. The fat columnist presented his stomach, and the only thing that you could reach over it was his extended hand. In contrast, the former soccer player thrust forward his battered face and hid his bent body behind it. The only thing to do had been to kiss that face.

I sniffed.

A few months later I was walking home late in the evening, and I saw the blue light of the television flicker through my friend's window. She opened the door and immediately poured me a whisky. On the floor next to the sofa stood an empty wine bottle. Feyenoord against Rapid Wien, she said. She had looked forward to the game all day; in the morning before leaving she had chilled a bottle for it, and within two minutes it had been over.

I think she said three–nil. Too far behind to catch up. Everything went wrong, and it rained cats and dogs on

the field. She had considered making the evening pro-
ductive: a free evening, she could read a book or write.
Paralysed, she had remained seated in front of the TV with
the bottle. All players with single-syllable names should get
out she said. Heus, Bosz, Maas, Vos, away with them. A chain
of syllables should be placed in defence to block any ball:
Schui-te-man, Bo-a-teng, Zwij-nen-berg. The miracle of disappointment had not yet been revealed to her.

I became busy and didn't see her for a time. Once in a
while I read newspaper reports about the European championship. It seemed to me that the performance of the
Dutch team could deliver ample material for the disappointment research that my friend was doing. Disappointment
is about loss, I thought. All loss is gain, but how? Your
heavy camera of three thousand guilders crashes down into a
ravine, and you walk up the mountain, nimble and relieved.
Unsuspecting, you storm into the bedroom where your lover
lies in bed with a stranger. You blow up your house with
everything in it and, liberated, you start a new life. Should
you see disappointment as a challenge and continue striving
in the same direction? Or was it instead a licence for change?
Could Feyenoord change into a successful fish market? It
couldn't be that simple. He had been pulling her leg, that
injured soccer player. I didn't understand it at all.

The summer was over. Together with all women over fifty in the neighbourhood, I received a summons from the Health Service to have my breasts examined at the expense of the state. This was to take place in the "Breast bus" which was parked at the entrance of the big hospital. The floor wobbled almost imperceptibly when I climbed in. A woman dressed in restful green was jammed behind a tiny reception desk in the waiting room. Handel's *Largo* sounded from loud-speakers. The waiting women sat talking with one another in hushed voices. The door to the examination area opened and my friend slipped into the waiting room. She looked at me and pointed at the loudspeaker. We both burst out laughing at the funeral music. She waited until it was my turn, but when I came back, my breasts flattened, she had disappeared. The woman in green lied that the photos hadn't come out right, that they had to be retaken; my friend had been taken in again.

When she finally reappeared, she was pale and gave the impression of being withdrawn. In her hand she held a folder with photos and papers, and she motioned me to come outside. We climbed down the narrow steps out of the bus. Outside, the autumn sun shone on the new soccer stadium. She said that something wasn't right; she'd had to see the doctor in a tiny little office behind the X-ray machine. He had looked at the photos with concern and immediately referred her to the surgeon.

I walked with her into the hospital to look for the surgery clinic. My friend was admitted that same day and was operated on the next morning. I stayed with her as much as possible but didn't have the feeling that I was really in touch with her. She seemed almost fanatically concentrated on something that was taking place within her. She was in training, she said when I asked her if she was scared. For months she had practised disappointments as best she could, and now she was facing her test of strength. Piet de Vries, she mumbled, Sparta's left-winger. Finally allowed to go along with the Dutch team, flew to Bulgaria, 1953, lost 3–2. Afterwards just went on playing soccer. With a wide, innocent smile. I wondered when disappointment would turn into a kiss of death, but I said nothing.

The operation showed that the tumour was benign. My friend returned home and life resumed. Weeks went by without our seeing each other, and I had almost forgotten her disappointment training when one winter evening she was suddenly at my door. I saw immediately that she had changed. The preoccupied look had disappeared, and she really looked at me, like before. We drank wine and smoked at my kitchen table. When I asked how things were with her disappointment programme, she nodded and started to talk.

She had met the former soccer player at a party; in the middle of a room full of stomping music and steaming people, he had suddenly stood in front of her. That evening, he had said, do you still remember that terrible evening;

they both had to laugh and went to get a drink in a quiet corner. Certainly, of course she remembered; thanks to his comment she had learned to bear everything, she told him. His love of disappointment had kept her going for a whole year. The soccer player had stared at her, shocked.

"I could never have said that," he said. "I hate disappointments!"

They looked at each other for some time, without speaking.

The finals

Those French women are already starting to clean fish at eleven o'clock in the morning. From the shutters over the row of draining boards a mist of shower gel and perfume still drifts out. They take their knives, their scissors, their scale scrapers and attack the fish. Their compact flowered bottoms form an impenetrable wall. I don't have a chance. Wash the salad. But how? I should have a colander. Our neighbour looks over her shoulder, looks straight through me. She sticks the point of the scissors into the fish and cuts it open. Guts and blood fall into the wash basin, move with the water towards the drain. Could I be pregnant? It stinks here.

I can't fry fish, he says. He's right. All French camping

sites have an area for regular guests. Campers are set up like mobile homes, like houses. On the strip of land between the steps and hedges there are washing machines, refrigerators and stoves. We have to have dinner at noon, do as they do. Says he. Afterwards rest in the tent, when the day is hottest.

By now, the neighbour at the back has prepared the fire for the fish. He's wearing shorts of smooth, blue-grey fabric. It wrinkles at his crotch.

With the dripping lettuce in my hands I stand in front of the tent. I kneel under the awning, manage to turn on the gas burner at my first try and put the steaks in the frying pan. The fire roars like a hurricane, blocking out all other sounds. It eats at your face.

Suddenly he stands behind me with a baguette. Bare feet, hairy shins. I ask if he'll set out the plates; I turn the steaks, sweating over the pan.

Then we sit on either side of the camping table. Our tent is standing on a grassy embankment and we look down on the living complex of our neighbours at the back, who are both busy preparing their fish. The salad is wet; he doesn't comment. He reports that he's met a nice man at the bakery. The man is staying here with his family in a cabin tent; he has a cross-country vehicle and a television. French. She is our age, he a bit older; they have small children.

How do you know all that, have you been to their tent? I ask. He borrowed tools, a jack or wrench, I don't hear it exactly, so that he can finally repair the car, but I lean back in my camping chair and look at the mountains in the distance. Snow, cool air, ice. Don't I want to eat any more? He takes the left-over half of my steak. I hear his teeth crush the meat. He has taken off his shirt and rubs his chest, over pink childish nipples between the chest hair.

I get up and collect the dirty dishes in the basin. He says something, I look up—shall I do the dishes for you? he says. For me. He wants to go to the sink for me, hold the greasy knives under the tap for me, spray them with too much of a too strong-smelling cleaning product, neatly replace them in the dried plastic basin, for me, for me.

I shrug my shoulders and try to stand the glasses upright in the tray, next to the plates and the cutlery. I thought that I had cooked for us. He thinks that I cook for him. With a heavy head, with steps that are too big, I walk to the washing area. The dishes rattle in the basin which I hold close. Grease spots on my dress. I sniff and blink my eyes. For him, then. All this is planned and done for him. The meal, the red bikini, the wrestling in the tent at night. For him, not for us.

It is quiet at the sinks. We must have finished eating too quickly. The taps are turned on by pressing the knob but stop running in a few seconds. The sink in the corner has a normal tap that keeps running. I empty the basin and fill it with lukewarm water. I bend forward and put my face in it. Everything turns red before my eyes. Through my nose and my mouth I suck in water. You could drown like this. Then I straighten up, dripping, and grab the dishtowel. With the towel pressed against my cheeks, I sit down on the stairs that lead to the washing area, my arms on my knees. I place my right cheek on my arm and look in the direction of the swimming pool which lies to the left in the distance. Splashing water, boisterous children, bare-breasted mothers lying down flat. On the covered terrace next to the water, the men sit in a half circle around a television set that has been placed on the bar. It gives off a greenish light; from my position I can see only movement, no image. From time to time the men get up from their chairs simultaneously and start a yell that ends in a sigh when they sit down again. There is a coarse chicken wire fence around the lawn with the reclining women. Two small children have hooked their fingers in the iron diamonds and peer through the screen.

I can ask, can't I? Why do you say such a thing, why do you want to do the dishes for me? Then he'll look at me sidelong, a bit weary. Just because, he'll say. Summer, someday, sunny, sonny, sun, sun, sun. Like that. I press the dishtowel against my eyes. Footsteps. He's coming to get me. I don't look.

Blind people hear much better than those who can see. They hear a child draw a circle, figure out the menu from the noisy eaters and distinguish weight, sex and type of shoe of passers-by. It's not him.

In the structure behind me doors are being slammed. Someone lets water splatter. Two women's voices speak loudly to each other, in short sentences.

Vacation means washing. Dishes, clothes, bodies. Everything is soaped up and held under a stream of water. Meanwhile you have to shout as in a conversation during a hurricane.

—If only I were dead.

—I can't get that grease spot out.

—Tonight I'm going to hang myself.

—I wanted to cook kidneys.

And so on, and so on. Idle talk.

203

He had the feeling that he'd been here before, he said the first evening as we sat contented on the chairs in front of the taut tent. That view. As if he were home. He looked across the expanse of grass, saw the people eating, the bathing suits hanging down from stretched guy lines, the children playing. We're staying here, he said.

We walked to the village to eat there on a terrace by a fast-flowing river. A silent boy with dull skin served us one dish after another, for a song, he said. I drank and drank. Couples wearing hiking boots sat around us. Inside, a French family pushed tables together and began a cheerful gathering.

Later I took the flashlight to go and brush my teeth in the washing shed. He peed in the bushes and was already in the tent when I returned.

When you are with a man, you are always with the three of you, because as soon as you leave for a moment, he's busy with his penis. He expects you to be interested in this hidden third one as well. You have to invest energy in it, as he does. As long as you're eating on a terrace, you can imagine that you're just together. In a tent, during a warm summer night, that's no longer possible. The third one has crawled up from under the sheets and wants to join in. For you.

204

The two children who were standing by the swimming pool are walking across the grass. The girl, in a striped cotton dress, is wearing plastic flip-flops. She is holding her younger brother's hand. His fat legs, buckling slightly inward, end in chubby feet that are pressed into soft sneakers. The large, serious head is set on a small thin neck. They are silent; they don't look around and walk straight to a tent in the distance.

I lift my head and watch them. Normal children don't walk like that. Intimidated children, frightened children, whipped children—these walk so obediently and so silently in a straight line. I've seen that at the day care centre. I imagine that normal children run a bit, fall over, shout something, laugh, tease each other. But what do I know about normal children? I don't have them. I take care of other people's bruised and damaged children.

I arrive at the tent with the clean dishes. He is reading the sports paper in the bright sun, in his bathing trunks. Shouldn't we do something, take a walk, look at a village square, buy something? Do something for which you have to get dressed?

You have a spot on your dress, he says. You're tired. Take off those clothes and come and lie in the sun, just leave those pots and pans. He says. It's an olive oil spot, a sticky dark spot on the grey-green cotton. He's right, I look awful.

In the tent I look for detergent, a towel, shampoo, another dress, a comb. So many things, they lie in a circle around me while I kneel on the ground. I smell the tent smell: camp scent mixed with sweaty sheet, a hint of rubber, a whiff of mowed grass. There's a nagging pain in my stomach. That's camping stress. I shouldn't whine so much. Rinse everything off under the shower. Let the spot soak in a bucket. Be relaxed. Remain calm.

In the empty wash area I look for a shower stall that hasn't got dirty water spilling over its ledge. I undress and stuff all my things in the plastic bag that I hang on the door hook. Before stepping into the square shower stall, I pull the iron chain and let the water splash straight down. With my foot I feel it slowly getting warm. Then I bend my head as I stand under the jet. I let the water run into my ears. I wash my hair, rub my body with soap and then pull the chain again with both hands. The water bubbles and tingles on my skin. To remain standing like that, balanced.

Through the water bubbles in my ears I hear a vague banging. Someone is yanking doors open and slamming them shut again. A dark voice utters a muffled curse. A man in the women's section, a cleaner perhaps? Then the whimpering sound of a child's voice. Horror-stricken, I forget to maintain the pressure on the tap. In the sudden quiet the man whispers threateningly, wild thumping and banging of limbs against wood can be heard, a tap is turned on, the water pipe bangs and the girl screams no, no, no.

My knees give way and I reach above my head to turn the shower on again. I crawl under the curtain of water as if it were a down comforter and for a moment I hear nothing more. Soap drips into my eyes and makes them tear. The child cries too; she rattles the door. The man's voice begins to hush, to cajole, to croon. I have to warn the supervisor, the campsite manager, the police. Or start screaming now that it has to stop, I'm coming, stop, cut it out, I'll kill you!

But I don't move. If I didn't hold onto the shower chain I would faint. If I didn't sit with my bare bottom on the tile floor, I'd fall over. The unintelligible supervisor who makes daily rounds on a patched-up moped, looking around for illegal rubbish and tents set up in the wrong way; the campsite manager who, swaying his stocky, hairy body from one leg to the other, rolls around behind his desk covered with picture postcards, forever raising his hands to avert administrative chaos and to refer the impatient guests to his wife; the police chief in his small palace at the end of the village who will stick his chin in the air and won't understand what I'm saying?

I let gallons and gallons of water run over my bent head. Until the child sobs softly and the man murmurs tender, approving phrases. Until doors swing shut, plastic rustles, footsteps fade away.

Then I dry myself slowly and get dressed.

We are going to visit his new friends. He has put on bermuda shorts and a short-sleeved shirt. Wrench in hand, he is waiting for me. The old French couple has sat down in their lounge chairs. Side by side, husband and wife are watching how we prepare for the visit. Their grill is shiny again; the dishtowel is hanging on the clothesline.

He places his hand on my back and kisses me on my wet hair. Then we walk straight across the yellowish grass to the farthest corner of the grounds where an enormous frame tent stands half under the trees.

I'm not very good at visiting. He is; he shakes hands,

accepts a drink and admires the view. He lets himself be patted on the shoulders by our host and is led to the monster truck that is parked next to the tent. I also get a hearty handshake and a glass of wine. Over his fat shoulders the host calls to his wife who is wiping the plastic windows of the tent with a wash rag. She walks with short steps on high-heeled mules without falling out of them. Sighing, she puts away the cleaning gear in the back of the tent. She reappears and places a perfectly ironed white cloth on the formica table. She sets cheese puffs, rolls with pâté, and intricately folded napkins on it. Without smiling she shows me a chair.

The men sit down right in front of a large television set that stands in the tent door. Social intercourse, meet new people, good for us. But for him it's about the semi-finals.

After every sip the hostess tops up my glass. I slouch back in the chair and drink. Maybe I close my eyes for a moment; I hear the rumbling of the men against the background of soccer noise. When I wake with a start, I see the children, the wandering pair, sitting in front of the television with cups of lemonade in their hands. On the screen a muscular black man in an orange shirt runs at full speed towards the goal. He is brought down and slams against the ground. No, no, no! the girl calls out. Her father snarls something at her; she is upset and he places his large hand on her shoulder. She moves away from him and puts her head on her knees.

That voice. So that's how it is. Sidelong I look at our

hostess. Her face expresses nothing. Unmoved she looks at the man, the way he sits there on the cheap camping chair, in sweatpants, with an open shirt, a hairy stomach and a bloated face. Good, he says, that'll teach that coffee bean.

Because I have drunk so much I know just what my hostess is thinking. She doesn't need to say anything. Fat slob, you only wish you had a fraction of the zeal, the elegance, and the force of that coffee bean. Clod. Keep your paws off me. That's what she's thinking.

I'm thinking that I don't want to be here any more, but because of the wine I feel very heavy. My tongue is paralysed but I see everything. The referee has stepped into the breach for the black man and holds a red card up to the opponent. Like grebes they rub their chests together. A large young man with a pale, egg-shaped face takes a penalty kick and shoots the ball into the goal, bang in the middle. Our host sniffs scornfully, but the others applaud and cheer. I drink to it.

He would be a sweet father if we had children. Just look how nicely he plays with the host's children. He stands in the goal between the posts of the ground's enclosure; he lets the small boy with the knock knees shoot at him time after time. He involves the girl in the game too; carefully he kicks the ball to her when she comes to watch. I empty my glass and let it be refilled. I hear him talk. He teaches them the names of the players: Van Gastel, Van Gobbel,

De Goey. For the first time this afternoon I look at the hostess; I toast her. The children get the giggles and shout out: Gassele-Gobbele-Goo!

Later he sits down again by the host; they want to drink. The man with the stomach motions his wife and points to the glasses. Camping does nothing for him, he does it for the children, year after year, so that they can be by the swimming pool in the clean mountain air. He himself is ready to go back to the city. He calls out to the children that they have to be careful with the ball; you have to be strict with the little ones so that they know how to behave and are no bother to anyone, he says.

Giggling, the children whisper to each other: Gasse-Gobbe-Goo, Gasse-Gobbe-Goo. The sun sets surprisingly fast behind the mountains. Now the light is losing its sharpness, I feel the skin around my eyes relax. I look at the landscape critically. The mountains stand like folding screens around terrible secrets: lost hamlets where dirty old men do unspeakable things in sagging sheds and cellars. The freshly-topped mountain ranges hide everything, like walls in a shower area. A secretive landscape, haughty and sly.

I have to tell her that the man is molesting the girl because I have heard it; I recognized their voices. She ought to know. The air stands between us like a wall. I can't speak.

Night has come and gone again. I lay sweating on my back in the tent; I didn't want to see the naked man next to me; I refused to open my eyes. He is gone when I wake in full daylight. If only I had a towering belly now, a belly that rose up from the sheets like a mountain and screened off all trouble. No one would be able to injure a hair on that child in that belly; no sound would be able to penetrate that safe darkness. I would put my hands against the sides; at a proper distance I would caress the child, kneed its little feet. And then make time stand still.

On my knees I crawl out of the tent; a half-filled bucket of water falls over. The ground is so dry that the moisture cannot soak in; it streams like a bulging rivulet towards the sleeping bag. I let it go. Because I really have to pee I'm forced to go to the washing area. There is such a racket that my pricked-up ears can't catch any trouble.

Freshly washed and combed, he receives me with coffee and bread when I return. He talks, he chatters, he prattles. Because Holland has won so weakly, so feebly, tomorrow the finals will be a contest between us and the French. He reports that the camp manager has rented a gigantic television screen so that the campsite population can watch the game together on the cement dance floor. The camp manager's wife is phoning in long lists of orders in her office; volunteers are helping with the installation of flags and decorations, and there will be a brass band and fireworks of course.

And I should go to the swimming pool to let my breasts get tanned.

I trudge there and lie down on a towel on the grass. I keep my t-shirt on. Everything hurts, my whole body is bloated and filled with fluid. I lie on my stomach, with my chin on my folded hands. Our hostess of yesterday sits in a low deck chair a few feet from me. She is wearing a bikini bottom and sunglasses. She turns her head in my direction but gives no sign of recognition.

The children, fully dressed, stand hand in hand at the edge of the swimming pool. They look at the other side, at the bar which is being decorated with garlands of coloured lamps between which portraits of soccer players are being hung. When the woman calls them, they come and stand next to the deck chair. The girl looks at her feet. The woman points at the water; the children shake no. Then they go off again, together, silently.

I place my cheek on my hands and close my eyes. I would never let such small children wander over a camping area by themselves. Unless of course I knew they were in even greater danger in the tent. She doesn't know it, that woman. Mothers never know it, they're easy-going. Is she even their mother? Maybe she's the new woman who doesn't want to come between him and the children. Or is he the boyfriend who treats her daughter so nicely? I should tell her, I should sit down across from those neat little breasts and reveal exactly what I have heard. Then she can pick up her things and leave with the children.

If I were her, I would run away without saying anything. If he, if we, had a child and he, he . . . I would have
to run away in order not to kick him to death. But
I don't even have a child. I could kidnap their children.
First I'd have to know French better. I have a boyfriend,
that might scare the girl. I'd better not say anything, not
do anything, not think anything. I'm not her; I'm myself.
Day and night I do my best to oblige someone, and even
when I'm stiff with fear, running away doesn't enter my
mind. You stay where you are. If I had a child, then I
would dare.

A shadow over my face, a hand on my back. I see a
bare thigh sticking out of purple shorts. A smiling face, an
open mouth with moist teeth. I sit up.

They're going to the city, he and the host; they're
going to buy fireworks for the camping manager. Everyone
is counting on a French victory, but he's going to try and
stock up on as many orange rockets as possible. He doesn't
know how long they'll be gone; I should do my own thing;
I shouldn't dress so warmly, take off my shirt, just do it,
go ahead! He tries to pull the stuck t-shirt from my body;
I see the other standing next to the gate, spying from behind
the sunglasses, waiting for the unveiling. With both hands
I pull down the shirt. Then I cross my arms in front of my
chest. He shrugs his shoulders and looks at the tanned front
of our hostess.

He pauses at her chair. I hear him ask her where the
children are, if they shouldn't be swimming, that he'll come

and play soccer with them this afternoon, till later, good-bye. I no longer watch.

I'm reading by the tent with my feet on his chair, under the awning. Later, it's already afternoon, I see a man with purple swimming trunks walking in the distance near the office. He has a child by the hand, the little boy. My heart skips a beat. How can that be, isn't he in the city? But I don't think that there could be a second pair of such idiotic trunks. Panting, I run to the entrance. They're gone.

Towards five o'clock I walk to the village and look at photos in the small bookstore. Through the shop window I see the village square, a large terrace under the sycamores. He is drinking pernod at one of the white plastic tables; the girl is sitting on the chair next to him and pours more water into his glass. Striped dress, purple shorts. No one to be seen when I come outside.

I'm not thirsty, but maybe I should drink something too. You can go crazy from loss of fluid. I'm going to buy a bottle of spring water and drink it all. I'm going to shop for French food, cook, do my best. I should tell him everything, especially him. You're mistaken, he'll say, it's because you can't free yourself from your work, such a burden for you, all those pathetic children. Yes, you're right,

I'll say then. At night I'll become pregnant, for us, a child for us. Everything will be all right.

I wake up late and everything is grey. A heavy cloud hangs above the valley and I have a stomach ache. A light wind sucks at the withered leaves under the hedge. A thunderstorm day, a no-good day. I zip the tent back up; I crawl into the stinking sleeping bag.

Wash and get dressed, he says. We're going to the party area; we'll drink to victory in advance. In the mirror above the wash basin my face is a puffy mask without lines. I wash myself with icy cold water, but I don't succeed in steeling myself. I feel like an ill-defined blob. I blink my eyes as hard as possible and with my brush I pull violently at my hair. If I had a knife, I would press it against my skin.

215

The dance floor is covered with a canvas canopy. Under it stand tables on trestles. The wife of the camping manager has put out glasses and bowls of nuts. Her black curls stick to her face; she is steaming with exertion. Smiling she approaches, a serving tray filled with baguette slices covered with a brown pâté. Her husband's voice sounds through the loudspeakers; he calls on all the guests to come; it's a party; it's free and everyone is welcome.

A skinny man with greasy hair stands on a ladder and

is repositioning something on the television screen. It is as large as a film screen. Boys carry in rough-hewn benches that they place in a herringbone pattern. Unintelligible commands, creaking, rustling.

He takes my hand. Skin and bones dissolve in fleshy warmth. We stroll across the party area, greet our neighbours and look at the various groups of guests. Many of the permanent residents are already present. The men, wearing vests and berets, sit at the tables drinking red wine, and the women are talking to one another in circles on the dance floor. The large screen shows snow. The cloudy sky casts everything in a grey-violet light. I put my feet down but don't feel the ground very well. I try to put force behind it, to stamp. You're walking funny, take it easy, he says, I'll get you a drink. The migratory folk, the people who stay for a few days or weeks and then move on, consist of two kinds: foreigners and French. The latter move across the ground with self-assurance, as if they have already won the finals. They speak loudly; I hear exclamations and shouts of laughter. The Dutch are diffident today and try not to attract attention. Everyone is walking every which way as if in a poorly rehearsed dance. They get out of the way to let the boss through. He pushes a wheelbarrow in which there is a tub filled with alcohol. A national mountain drink, he shouts, good luck wine, a treat. With the help of his wife, he puts the tub on a stool next to the table with glasses. He stirs it vigorously with a soup ladle. The people crowd together in front of him when he starts pouring. The drink is a deep purple colour and smells vaguely of methylated spirits. In it float hard chunks: apple, unripe melon? I take a glass and do my best to finish it quickly.

The television link-up has been established. Players and coaches are moving their lips soundlessly. Accordion music comes from the loudspeakers. All the sounds reach me as if filtered through a layer of cotton batting. The manager's wife has hoisted a transparent jerry-can onto the table, and from it she pours lemonade for the children. I see the boy and the girl standing in front of her with serious faces, holding plastic cups in outstretched hands. A short distance away, their parents are drinking purple juice in a circle of Frenchmen. The accordion music stops to give way to an excited journalist's voice. The camera swings past a hundred thousand faces; over the poison-green grass the players, two by two, dash into the stadium. Applause. Carefully the two children walk with their cups from under the canopy. They listen to the anthem and look closely at the faces of the players who are being shown one by one. My hand is released and hangs in the air like a flake of foam. I see him standing next to the children; he bends towards them and points out the Dutch players: Van Gastel, Van Gobbel, De Goey. The children nod. Do try to smile now— them or me? The father comes towards me and offers me a glass of purple drink; he is holding his son by the hand. Where is the girl? And where is *he*? I shake my head and hurriedly start walking through the crowd. I look along the benches, I search near the drinks table and scour the dance floor several times. Nothing. Gone. I'm alone.

All eyes are directed at the screen, no one looks at me. Irritated, people move their arms when I nudge past them. I trip over stretched-out legs, start at the sudden shouting at a foul and am surrounded by stamping, cheering bodies when a goal is made. The noise is unbearable, the lights and the colours sting my eyes, the purple party drink pounds in my brain. A Frenchman enthusiastically jumping up and down steps on my foot; I have to get out of here; I feel the sweaty warmth coming off the people; I want water, water, peace and quiet.

It isn't until I'm near the washing area that I slow down. The outside light is broken but through the shutters the light of the fluorescent tubes falls on the path. The sinks glimmer palely in the half-light; there is a forgotten dishtowel, a brush, a fork. With my shoulder I push open the door; I drag myself inside. On the floor lie empty shampoo bottles and balls of pink toilet paper. I don't feel like looking in the mirror and immediately go into a toilet stall. Very still, I try to stand straight against the door. Breathe slowly now, feel the wood at my back, let my arms hang down, silent.

A tap drips. Shuffling. Smacking sounds, sniffing, a stifled outcry. I flush the toilet and slam the door but remain standing stock-still against the inside. I have to know. It is quiet. The only sound comes from outside: the soccer commentator, the screaming of the public, a pop of an early rocket.

I'm dizzy; I undo my pants and sit down on the toilet seat with my head in my hands. Then I hear it again: giggling, a rasping voice, Gastel, Gobbel, Goey? A shower is turned on, a child calls out surprised, a man laughs. The water splashes deafeningly in the empty space.

Look, I'm sitting here late in the evening on a toilet in a camping ground in France. I'm here with my boyfriend, we are on vacation, during the day we take walks in the mountains and at night we have a drink with people we meet. Relax, rest, nothing special. He loves children; he likes to watch how they play and likes to play with them. I'm less at ease; I'm not as good with people. He doesn't always have to look after me, that would be a nuisance for him. I never feel like doing anything. In the past things were not too nice for me, but I never speak about that because now I have everything: a job, a lover, a camping tent, and who knows, maybe even a child in my belly. I let him do his own thing; it's his vacation too; he must be able to do what he wants. But what does he want? He wants to lie on top of me, sweating; he wants to sit naked in the sun; he wants to be in the swimming pool with the children.

Suddenly I see it. When he makes love to me, he is thinking of the little girl. At every new camping ground he scans the tents for families with small children. I think that he is flirting with the mother; he's thinking of the daughter. He seems to be teaching her to kick a ball, but he's watching how her legs disappear under her skirt. That's it. If he wants a child, it's not for us. It's for him.

The blood has drained from my head and my throat is bone-dry. I would like to scream, but I can no longer make a sound. I know that I have to disappear, but I'm paralysed.

Spots in my panties. That explains my stomach ache. Again nothing. Think, make a plan. I have to go to the tent, put on clean clothes, grab a sweater, passport, money. And then away.

220   The air is clammy and hangs in grey wisps above the warm crowd of people. The television screen shows in close-up the face of a terrified man who is staring into the distance with a wild look. His upper lip is pulled up; between the hairs of the moustache his teeth glisten like a rabbit's. Then he opens his mouth; he screams and with a gloved hand he points somewhere, desperately.

Behind the people I steal to the tent. I see the lit-up guy lines and take care not to trip over them. Blindly groping I find clean panties, sanitary napkins, my sneakers, the wallet. I don't sit down to reflect; I'm in a hurry. Outside they cheer, but the panicked goalkeeper is probably crying. Where will I sleep? How do I get home? Don't think. You have to get to the exit; you have to get though the gate; you have to follow the narrow black road through the valley, to the north.

My breathing is quick and light. I bend my knees, stretch my arms above my head as if I'm loosening my muscles for a race. My skin contracts. Goosebumps.

I don't dare go past the dance floor again. I descend to the flat area of our neighbours at the back and sneak smoothly past the stove, around the trailer, to the flagstone path that joins the road leading to the gate.

I have to go past the washing area. Fortunately the lamp is broken. I walk on the grass in order not to make a sound. Something looms in the darkness of the entrance, a large body, an enormous hunchback. I hold my breath and keep walking, on tiptoe. In my trouser pocket my hand clasps the paper money and the credit card. One more street light, then the office and the exit. The shutter of the office is rolled down and there is no one in the telephone booth.

The hunchback approaches the light. His hump is no hump. It's a child's head. The large, round head of the little boy that lies crooked against the father's shoulder. I stand still, I don't move. The child looks at me and smiles. Gasse, Gobbe, Goo, he whispers. The father's large hand strokes his hair.

Past the gate I run up the road, past the garbage cans with their vague fish smell, ever farther from the frenzied cheering and the noise that rumbles from the dance floor through the valley. I count my footsteps and adjust my breathing until I find a rhythm that I can keep up for a long time. There is no moon, there are no stars.

Rockets and great showers of sparks light my way.

A harbour

"Perhaps you should first tell me what happened."

Roemer Te Velde, I said when she shook my hand at the door. She led the way upstairs, to a room which was as I had imagined it: a large chair for the therapist and opposite it a slightly smaller one for the patient. For me. For the rest I saw nothing, actually; I looked mainly at her.

She doesn't write down anything, she does nothing but listen very intently. Sleeping badly and lack of concentration, those I can talk about very well. Sudden, angry outbursts, an occasional crying fit which doesn't bring relief. Fear that I will jeopardize my training. Apathy, what do I care? And all that since . . . since that weekend, yes, since the thing happened that she is asking about, because I am procrastinating so frightfully, because I am steering clear of these intolerable things.

"We were going sailing for a weekend, my supervisor and I. I'm a resident with Dick Buikhuis, an orthopaedic surgeon. He has a boat in Durgerdam."

Early in the morning he picked me up. He sat honking in his Volvo station wagon, and I rushed down the stairs with a bag filled with raingear. It was glorious weather; clear sky, stiff breeze. He didn't look well, I thought; it was actually absurd to leave so early if you were that tired. But I did everything he said. I was ready at seven o'clock. I had already told him that I couldn't sail; it wasn't a problem. I was embarrassed when he rejected my shoes. I needed boat shoes, like his. He thought that I could probably borrow them from the harbourmaster.

"I don't know if you have ever sailed. There's a lot of fuss before you can actually leave; drag everything out of the car, remove and store tarps, draw ropes through pulleys. Hours of work. After that we went to a kind of shed, to the manager of the harbour."

A strange man in purple shorts. His shirt hung open even though it was not very warm. The man was playing table football with a group of little boys who took to their heels when we came in. Dick shook the man's hand, gestured casually towards me and asked for coffee. The man was just back from vacation and began telling us about it in great detail. He complained. Holland had lost the world soccer championship and his wife had left him, in one breath. He leaned over the bar and looked intently at Dick.

"Dick listened to his stories. He's always very friendly. I kept away from the two of them and thought about what still had to be done. I thought that man was unpleasant, strange."

All that complaining. And Dick as the understanding doctor. The water tank still had to be filled, the fuel checked, there was no time to sit and chat here. It was using up our time. I could borrow shoes with rubber soles. I don't have to say all that, do I? They talked about women. Dick is married; he has two daughters.

"When we came back to the boat, Enno had arrived, Enno Kallander, a fraternity friend of Dick, from Leiden. He was standing on the landing with two very heavy shopping bags, in impeccable casual clothes. Scarf in his polo collar, that kind of thing. A short little man. He's a famous art historian."

An old queer, I thought right away.

225

"You were disappointed?"

Because I wanted to be alone, alone with Dick she means. That's what I really wanted. I blush.

"I don't know. No, the boat was much too big for

that. To man it with just the two of us, I mean. I hadn't thought about it."

Already I'm lying. I *was* disappointed. I still remember that when I crawled into the cabin to put away the food, I banged my head against the hatch and tears came to my eyes. Dick and Kallander sat talking in the cockpit and slapping each other's knees. There were two berths in the cabin, and in the fore-cabin too. Yes, I was disappointed. I had looked forward to something that was not going to happen, although I didn't know what it was.

Kallander's figure darkened the cabin entrance. It was a tight squeeze when we both stood in the gangway. He shooed me upstairs; he wanted to arrange the provisions himself and make coffee. Dick was tinkering with the motor and sent me onto the landing to untie the lines.

"Finally we sailed away. With the last rope in my hand I had to jump on the afterdeck."

I hesitated. I jumped. The harbourmaster was waving us off, again surrounded by children. I couldn't help thinking of his vanished wife. How long did he wait for her, alone in the tent? Do you go to the police, do you go home, what do you do? And why didn't I ask?

"When we were on open water, Enno handed us mugs of coffee. Dick sat at the helm. We skimmed over small waves; meanwhile the sails were full, the wind was favourable and steady. Enno came to sit with us in the cockpit. There was a conversation about disappearances; I still remember that because it surprised me so. Dick talked about a difficult operation he had planned, the correction of a badly healed fracture; I can still remember the case. He said he was baffled when the patient simply decided against it, with a brief thank you, in a short note. I never knew that he had minded so much.

"Enno reacted very sympathetically and started a long story about a vanished painting. The only person who had ever seen it was no longer able to rediscover its location. He was consumed with annoyance but was powerless.

"I didn't say much, I just watched them. They looked old, these two men. Greying, tired, their backs slightly bent when speaking about their failed exploits. The harbour of Durgerdam disappeared in the humidity. The air was hazy, as Dick called it."

227

"They appealed to you, those stories about disappearance?"

Right away I see the kitchen before me, at home, when all of us still lived at home. My father in the doorway, on the way to his room, Biene and me quarrelling at the table. My mother at the stove. Her back.

"The fact that there's something there, that you count on without thinking, which suddenly disappears. That you continue to live while something is missing. Something like that. I think it's strange."

I must have thought that it was typical of children,

disappointment, rage caused by the disappearance of things, the cancellation of plans, the failure of an enterprise. Adults are not so powerless, they can carry through what they have planned to do. If something fails they have done it intentionally. That's what I thought. If a smart mother calls off an operation, it's because Dick steered her that way, that's how I see it. I was quite surprised by the fact that he was disappointed and offended.

Long before we were near the lock he had us lower the mainsail, without explanation. With a command. The canvas fell in folds onto me, I caught it with outstretched arms and tied up the sail ties with childish bows. We had exactly the right momentum to get us inside the open gates of the lock.

Wait. Chat with fellow skippers. Tie the boats to each other, fenders between them. Throw the loose lines over the bollards on the wharf.

"In the lock we sat down to eat. It took quite some time. Enno had made sandwiches with all sorts of exotic things on them: marinated mushrooms, roasted eggplant and Italian sausage. Dick went ashore to talk with the lock-keeper. I stayed behind with Enno."

"Yes?"

How does she mean: yes? Is she asking something or is it more a confirmation? She underlines what I say, maybe. I stayed behind with Enno. Yes.

"What he said about his work I found fascinating. A restoration is just like surgery: you have to formulate a plan of operation, make an estimate of what the patient, the painting, can handle; you work with materials that reject one another or instead establish a bond—there are many similarities. When you hear him talk like that, it's pure heroism, just as with us. Except with him it involves enormous sums."

It sounds as if I'm defending him.

"He has known Dick for ages, since college. He asked if I was also such a passionate doctor. He spoke very nicely about Dick; 'Dickey', he said, and how good it was that he now had a supervisory position and that he, Kallander that is, thought that there was a good chance for a professorship. He thought Dick was working too hard and asked what I thought about that. It's normal, I said, it goes with the job."

It's only when you're dizzy with fatigue that you feel like a real doctor.

When Dick came back on board I could see that he was exhausted. Despite the sun, his skin was almost greyish in colour, and he sighed a lot. But he was happy when the lock gates opened and he pushed us off with the hook. Bent over the stick which he had placed against the wall of the lock, he walked slowly aft from the bow, gasping. He held the whole weight of the boat in the palm of his hand.

Sailing is the most beautiful thing, he said. You ruin it completely if you turn on the motor.

"On the IJsselmeer the wave-action is tricky. You don't notice it much, there are no big waves or anything. Still, after sailing for a while, there is a nagging feeling in your stomach. 'You look green,' said Dick, 'you have to eat a lot and keep busy.' He sent me forward to trim the jib. I held on to the mast and looked across the water. I breathed slowly and deeply. The nausea disappeared. I saw the two men sit together, Dick at the helm and Enno looking up at him."

It flashed through my mind that I could jump overboard and that Dick would go after me, save me. Ridiculous. His arm around my neck. Idiotic.

"The sky had become overcast; actually we moved forward between water and clouds. You didn't see land anywhere. I walked carefully to the cockpit. Enno went inside, he was cold. Not Dick, he had rolled up the sleeves of his sweater so that you could see his large blond forearms on which the veins branched off like rivers. We talked about the department; he asked if I thought my talents were being used fully there. It reduced me to silence; it was a fatherly type of question. I always feel anxious when someone is so nice to me. I didn't know what to say and thought he would find me stupid. A failure. A disappointment."

She is sitting there with her legs crossed and her arms on the arms of the chair. Beautiful shoes she's wearing. Shouldn't she be asking me now if I feel like a failure here too? She does nothing but look. My eyes sting. Don't cry now, control yourself, there's nothing wrong. I should just continue telling the story.

"The wind came slightly from behind. Dick had fastened the clew of the mainsail and the helm as well. No one had to do anything. We got up a good speed."

It is not unusual for someone to feel like a fool in the presence of his supervisor. Also you then imagine all sorts of heroic deeds which will make that supervisor admire you. But I thought: help me, save me. That's ridiculous.

"I no longer remember exactly what happened then. I felt awful and wasn't really paying attention. It was rather still on the water. Enno was rummaging in the cabin. Dick pointed out a small boat to me, to our right, a small craft with two or three people in it. I grabbed the binoculars and tried to catch sight of them, to have something to do, to hold something in front of my eyes."

She nods. She shifts position.

231

"I saw a broad-shouldered young man who had thrown his arm around a very thin blond girl. Another girl, dark and sturdy, held the helm. I saw their mouths moving; they were laughing and were drinking beer from bottles. I had an acute desire to sit in the boat with them; it looked so good, so companionable.

"Dick loosened the helm and the sail again in order to be able to manoeuvre. It was fairly windy and the small boat was swiftly coming closer. It was my task to haul on the clew to hold the sail taut. Dick changed course slightly to give the other boat more room. He pulled the helm towards himself with both hands. His back was touching mine, I felt him become heavier and heavier. I moved aside. He hit the floor. I was frightened, let the rope slip, I think I screamed. The sail started flapping and the boom swung back and forth over our heads with a creaking sound. Or had the boom hit Dick on his head? The clew hung in the water. What was I supposed to do?"

I rub over my face. I can't even recount clearly what happened. What did *not* happen. How I stood hesitating for seconds whether to bring the boat back on course or worry about Dick. How I, a doctor, was scared when I looked at him. How I let him, wide-eyed, claw at his sweater without doing anything myself. How he keeled over surprisingly slowly onto my feet. It was only then that I woke up, more or less.

"I let go of the sail and tugged at Dick until he lay stretched out along the bottom of the cockpit. Enno stuck his head out of the hatch. I shouted to him to watch the sails. He climbed over Dick and walked to the front. I took Dick's hand but couldn't feel a pulse, not even in his neck. I pushed his sweater up, looked for the bottom of the sternum and started pushing. I sat straddling the body and my knees bumped against the benches but I felt no pain. I should give him artificial respiration, I thought. Push three more times, then blow. His head lay against the steps to the cabin. I clamped his nose closed and placed my lips around his mouth. I blew."

How I lay over him. Chest on chest. Mouth on mouth.

"Then I pumped again, with extended arms. I concentrated on the rhythm and counted. Suddenly there was an enormous crash which sent a shudder through the boat and almost caused me to fall over. I heard splitting wood, screaming, the sound of heavy objects plunging into the water. The stays crashed against the mast. I kept counting and blew when I had to blow, with my eyes closed. I didn't want to think of anything else. My trousers grew wet, Dick had let his urine pass. I kept ramming against his chest wall while the boat rolled horribly.

"A soaking wet girl came aboard over the gangway; it was the helmsman of the small boat. Blow, I said. I pointed at the cabin entrance, she should kneel there so that she could give artificial respiration to Dick without being in my way. Push five times, then straighten my back for a moment while she did her work. The small sail lay on the water, the small boat was already half sunk. Junk floated around: plastic bags, a yellow raincoat, and our life buoy. I bent over his chest again."

Out of the corner of my eyes I saw the boy in his soaked clothes crawling over the seat to the helm. He scrabbled around for the ropes and tried to get the ship back under control. He said nothing. The noise came from the thin girl; she stood screaming next to the mast while the water dripped from her shorts. Her legs were so thin that you could see the shape of the skeleton. I started. My attention remained glued to that emaciated body. Then I thought of the person dying between my legs. With all my might I tried not to think of my helper. Every time I rested from the strong pushing movements, she bent towards Dick's head; I saw her nipples hanging in the wet sweater and waited for the moment when she would enclose his mouth with her lips. With one hand she held his nose closed, the other pressed lightly on his chin so that the mouth fell open. Open. It took place eight inches away from my face; I couldn't help but look, excited, and therefore confused. Then I myself lay over him again as if I wanted to push myself straight through his chest. It was as if via Dick's body we were touching each other, holding each other, biting each other. Something was happening that couldn't happen, that shouldn't happen at all.

"You're very quiet?"

"She was very good, that girl. She knew how to do it and she wasn't afraid. We continued for a long time; I didn't want to stop. I couldn't stop. I checked the pulse regularly, but it wasn't there. At least half an hour elapsed before we looked at each other and nodded. He was dead.

"I straightened myself, incredibly stiff. The squares of the woodwork of the floor were imprinted on my knees. My arms were trembling and I felt bruised right there under my thumbs—what's it called, the ball of the thumb. I heaved myself onto the bench. She sat down on the stairs and lay her head on the sill. Her wet, black hair fell over her arm. It was over."

I felt a sort of compassion for the wet girl who had helped me so well. I wanted to stroke her hair but was too badly numbed to be able to move.

"I kept thinking: he is dead, I have to do something. Now I was the only doctor on board."

"And what you had done didn't help."

"No. Yes. I wondered where Kallander was; he turned out to be sitting in the cabin with the skinny one. My helper turned around and went inside too. I called out that she should put on my extra clothes, from the bag standing on one of the berths inside. After a while she reappeared and climbed carefully past Dick's head. She sat down next to me. There was really no place for our feet, so we kind of pushed them against the body. She was wearing my socks.

"'I'm Hanna,' she said. 'The one inside is Noor, she's all upset, but that man calmed her down.' The head and shoulders of the skinny one appeared and disappeared again.

She was wearing silk pajamas, she looked at the young man who was steering the boat in silence and said nothing. Later, Enno came upstairs.

"When he saw Dick lying there, he mumbled something like: no, no, this cannot be. I gave him a hand very awkwardly, to help him into the cockpit, but it looked as if I were offering my condolences. I was ashamed, I was completely mortified, frankly. Enno behaved like a real friend. He placed his hands on each side of Dick's face and tried to press the eyes closed. That didn't really work; they kept opening a crack so that you saw a shiny stripe of white of the eye. Meanwhile tears trickled down Enno's cheeks. Distressed, he sat down across from us. 'We should cover him up,' he said, 'in any case.' He took his glasses from his nose and wiped his face.

"'The jib,' said the young man at the helm in a surprisingly low voice, 'you can take the jib down.' Hanna was already walking to the front and I followed. We released the sail from the stay and the clew and carried it to the cockpit."

I saw her buttocks moving in my own jeans, under my own sweater. My knees hurt terribly, I could just sink through them, slide into the water.

"We covered Dick with the sail. The four of us sat around him, secretly pushing our feet under the body because there was no other room. Enno had put Nora down to sleep in the fore-cabin. 'That seemed best to me,' he said. His voice sounded slightly unsteady. The young man at the helm, clearly her fiancé or her boyfriend, thanked him. She couldn't take very much yet, she had just come out of the hospital, he said. They had gone to his parents in Lelystad, where he had grown up; with Hanna, their friend, they had rented a boat to go sailing for an hour, to distract her, he had thought. That had pretty well succeeded, I thought: a shipwreck, a heart attack, a dead person on board. You wouldn't be thinking about food.

"The boy sat shivering and I realized that he was still sitting in the wind with sopping wet clothes. Hanna took over the helm and I went below with Jelle—that was his name, Jelle Beuling; he introduced himself properly in the cabin, even shook my hand. Enno didn't seem to be planning to part with any more clothes after his generous gift to the skinny one, and I had nothing else. I found overalls, waterproof boots and a raincoat. Belonging to Dick.

"Nora couldn't stand dead people; her father had died of a mysterious illness when she was still very young. It made her panic, said Jelle, while he stood in his bare ass between the berths. In his new clothes he stumbled to the fore-cabin. I picked up the wet mess from the floor and put everything into the plastic shopping bags that Enno had saved. Between the cabin and the fore-cabin was only a curtain. I heard Jelle whispering and the girl crying softly.

"Oh well. After some time we all sat upstairs again. Except for Nora, that is. The wind had died down and it became increasingly foggy. Enno had recovered and had gone to make us something to drink in his gimballed galley. That's what it's called. It was as if all of us thought at the same time: what now?

"'We have to let his wife know as soon as possible,' Enno said through the hatch. Jelle thought of the man who had rented them the sunken boat and Hanna wanted to inform the police. No one had brought a phone. I moved the jib to the side and, leaning over awkwardly, I started to feel in Dick's pockets because I knew that he had one. The skin looked yellowish, and the body had perceptibly cooled. I tried not to look at his face and replaced the sail as soon as I had found what I was looking for.

"It didn't work. You had to punch in a code which we didn't know.

"'What's that thing called,' said Jelle, 'for sending. A ship-to-shore radio. There's got to be one on a boat like this!'

"The cabin smelled of cocoa. Enno and I found the apparatus. No one knew how to work it. While Enno was stirring the pan, I knelt in the berth and fiddled with the knobs. I asked Enno to turn off the gas and heard a noise, a hissing from an immense space. It was pointless; I didn't know how to make the apparatus transmit, and I had no idea of the frequency used by the water police or any one else. At random I pushed keys and knobs until suddenly an affected man's voice broke loose out of the thing: 'because beauty has something to do with economy. The movements of the dancer are of an exalted physical beauty and also very economical, just like the movements of a soccer player. Personally I would like to choreograph a number of soccer players; that seems a marvellous challenge with dazzling potential, for the public as well.'

"'Stop that!' another voice shouted. 'Did I come from my fireside for this nonsense? Stop that! I'm leaving!'

"I turned off the apparatus. In the cabin they were drinking in silence. Enno had poured good-sized shots of cognac into the mugs of hot chocolate."

"You describe all that happened so exactly, but what did you actually feel?"

"Not much. I thought primarily about what would happen next, how we would get to land, and where, and what would follow then in telephoning and arranging. Practical things, that's what I thought about. I don't think I was sad or anything. Rather numbed."

And in love, but I don't dare to say that. I was thinking of Hanna's naked body, slowly warming up in my clothes. Of her mouth, right before she blew her breath into Dick. Of her hand around his chin and his neck. I was intent on figuring out ways to meet her again later; I could see her pottering about in my kitchen without clothes, lying in my bed. That's what I thought while I sat by my deceased instructor. I wanted to be rid of all these people. Piss off,

239

that hysterical Nora with her boyfriend. Enno shouldn't
have been there at all, right from the start.

"A burial at sea. We could roll him into the jib and
lift him. With the four of us it would work. And then let
him slip overboard."

Now it's out. The image of a white bag disappearing
in water and fog hangs between us. I've said it out loud.

"People think all sorts of things in such a situation," she
says calmly. "Trivial, strange and embarrassing things.
That's how it is. Probably you were also just plain irritated
that your weekend was ruined."

240 As if I didn't have enough on my mind, yes. As if without
asking they could force on me balding art historians, cardiac
decompensations and anorexic drowning persons. I was
entitled to a few days of freedom and rest but was saddled
with impossible tasks and a feeling of total inferiority. I
had done nothing right. I had snubbed Enno, let Dick
die, been unable to turn on the ship-to-shore radio. To get
back to land, I was dependent on a young man in dead
man's clothes, for I couldn't sail either. She has a box of
paper tissues there. Blow my nose. Rub my eyes. Breathe
deeply.

"During the resuscitation I had kicked the compass
to pieces. We didn't know where we were. Originally Jelle

had planned to sail back to Lelystad but he preferred to be pushed by the wind. It had been a westerly wind, and perhaps it still was. You couldn't see a damn thing, we were kind of drifting about. I was afraid it would get dark. No one said anything. That made it more scary. And the fact that I really didn't know any of these people. I didn't know what they were thinking; I knew nothing at all, and I really can't stand that. Whiteness. Clouds everywhere. I became increasingly detached from everything.

"I can barely remember how we reached the shore. Jelle was babbling about Urk, I think, but that didn't appear on our horizon. It wasn't until it was dark that we saw a light somewhere and could set course for it. I hadn't thought of that in my stupidity. Finally we ended up in a sort of canal, very wide, with deserted land on both sides. Naturally no one was able to turn on the motor, and we were dependent on the evening wind. So it didn't exactly go fast.

"Enno became very nervous and started poling once we were in the channel. From time to time I heard Nora shouting in the forecastle: 'Dead, he is *dead*!' I was sailing on a ship of fools. I sat down with my back to the cabin and my feet on the bench; I looked back over the water and kept out of everything."

"What do you still remember of the arrival?"

"That Kallander started to shout. Perhaps I had dozed off for a moment because it startled me awake. That he saw a church on a hill, with two naves, late Gothic, exceptionally unusual and interesting. He remained the expert.

"We were in Vollenhove. Police came on board. They shone a flashlight over the boat and stooped to inspect the stem. There was a penetrating smell of smoked eel; I still remember that I was hungry. And that Dick was placed on a stretcher and driven away in a hearse. Enno and I were questioned at the police station. Interrogated I should say. I refused to call my father and didn't want them to either.

"That night we slept in a hotel. From my room you could see the harbour and the eel smokehouse near where the boat was moored. That night I slept well."

She is silent. Time must be almost up. I still haven't said anything, not really, and soon I'll be back on the street.

242   "What happened to the others?"

Now. This is the last chance. Would you rather be blind or deaf, I used to ask Biene when we were small; would you save your father or your mother if the house were burning? She would shake her head until the tears flew everywhere.

If I say something now, she'll have me admitted, and if I'm silent I may come back for useless therapy.

I am still in this cloudlike state. I look at my thoughts as if at an X-ray. During the day I measure parts of bone and move joints. I write down what patients tell me and make notes of the medicines that I administer. But in the evening. But at night.

I look at the woman.

"Maybe there are no others," I say. "Maybe I just imagined it, that the others were there. Dick is dead. We went with the whole department to the funeral. We really did sail because the boat shoes are standing at the back of my clothes closet. At the cemetery I saw Kallander; he avoided me, therefore he exists. I haven't told you that my mother has been admitted to the psychiatric hospital."

I rattle on. Anything to prevent her saying: oh, is it like that, what did you get into your head, go and get a pill in the outpatient clinic and don't bother me with your hallucinations. To put off her saying: of course you're crazy, someone who reacts so impassively to such a terrible loss, I can't help him, I don't want anything to do with him.

I would really like to leave now. Grab my coat from the coat rack downstairs and walk down the street at a brisk pace. I'm very warm in here.

"Do you think that you imagined reinforcements because you were facing this alone?"

I think of the harbour master, in his purple shorts. A broken, unpleasant and lonely man, surrounded by a cheerful band of little helpers. Help, yes, reinforcements. A strong, firm yet sensitive young man to sail the boat to a harbour. A sweet and foxy woman to save Dick. A tawny, raving mad witch to wail when that failed. I got help because I needed help. For the first time during this hour I notice that my chair has a comfortable back. I stretch my legs and sigh.

"If that's the case, we'll figure it out." She picks up a large appointment book from her desk.

"Shall we continue next week?"

About the author

Anna Enquist
Photo by Vincent Mentzel

Anna Enquist, a psychoanalyst and classically trained musician, was born in 1945. A few years ago she began to write poetry, as she said, 'from one day to the next'. Today, she is one of the Netherlands' most popular poets and novelists, with a large readership in Germany, Switzerland, Austria and Sweden.

The Toby Press has published her first and second novels, *The Masterpiece* and *The Secret*. Both have sold over 200,000 copies in the Netherlands, and *The Secret* was chosen by Dutch readers as the Book of the Year in 1997.

The fonts used in this book are from the Garamond and Akzidenz Grotesk families.